MEGAN

Breadcrumbs For The Nasties
Book One

STEVEN NOVAK

QUIET CORNER

Cover design by Steven Novak

www.novakillustration.com

ISBN: 061585947X
ISBN-13: 978-0615859477

For my wife

1

Mother died when I was ten. Father figured it was something she'd eaten—tainted meat from any one of the expired cans we'd been surviving on. Truthfully, I don't think he had any idea what took her from us. Looking back, I suppose it didn't matter. Even if he had known, it wouldn't have changed anything. There was no way to help her. The sickness had its way with her. It ate her slowly. It was patient, took its time, enjoyed itself. Her fingernails dried and peeled away. Her skin turned to paper. When I touched her, she recoiled and winced. She was so sensitive. Breezes became uncomfortable, droplets of rain like tiny nails against her flesh. Her eyes glossed over, blurred into clouds, milky and white. Her hair fell away, handfuls left on the road as we traveled. Father made a point to stop and bury as much as he could.

Breadcrumbs for the nasties. That's why he said we couldn't just leave it out in the open: *breadcrumbs for the nasties.*

While I wasn't fully aware of the breadcrumb reference, I believe I understood the basics. *They* would smell the hair the same way they smelled everything. They would smell the hair, and it would lead them right to us.

By the third week of her sickness, mother's face had transformed into something wrinkly and crumply, whisper-thin and so very delicate. Her eyes sank into their sockets, the surrounding flesh like old leather. The color of her pupils was gone. It had dulled and washed out, a milky nothing. Her hands were an awful purple-blue, bruised and blotchy. Her lips cracked, but refused to bleed. She was so beautiful once, my mother, so very beautiful. I wanted to look like her. I wanted to walk like her and smile like her. I wished I had her dimples.

I loved her dimples.

At night, lying beside her as she stroked my face, father standing watch, I would count the awful blue veins creeping up her arm like dried tree branches— more of them every day. Every night it took longer. When she looked down at me and tried to smile, I could tell she wanted to cry.

She never did.

At no point in my life can I recall seeing mother cry. There were opportunities of course, many of them. She could have cried. I wouldn't have thought any less of her. A part of me believes it was because of me. She didn't want me to see. Tears were a luxury, and luxury was a word that no longer held meaning. My mother was a strong woman, right to the end.

Thirty days after she originally fell ill, just before sunset, she died.

I remember the moment distinctly. I'll never forget it. I don't want to. She dropped to the dirt and began to shake. Her knees tucked in close to her chest and her skeleton arms wrapped around them, fingers bent and frozen. Her wrists twisted inward, broken nails clawing at the fabric of her jacket as if salvation were hidden among the folds. When she opened her mouth, no sound emerged. Her face was a scream. Her breath was a whisper. Father lifted her in his arms and carried her to the trees. I wanted to follow. I wanted to help him carry her. I wanted to unfasten her jacket and tear it from her body to stop her from sweating. I wanted to mash the palm of her hand against my face and let her know I was there. I wanted to kiss her crinkled skin and sob into the crook of her neck. Instead, I did nothing. I couldn't move. From twenty feet away I watched, hands shoved in my pockets and tears in my eyes as father beat on her chest and screamed her name. He opened her mouth and huffed into her throat. Then he did it again. For a full ten full minutes, he repeated the process, until his arms were spent and his lungs hollow. He tried everything, everything he could possibly try. And then he tried it again. In the end, it didn't matter. When no options remained his head slumped forward, shoulders limp. Broken, he buried his face in the hollowed cavity of her chest, wrapped his arms around her body, and screamed.

I'm not sure what he said. It wasn't meant for me.

I remember the moment my mother died so clearly—too clearly. To this day, I can recall the look on father's face, eyes soaked, tears spread like lightning down his cheeks. I'd never seen my father cry, either. I'd never seen it before and would never see it again.

Fifteen minutes later, he was done.

From the road, I watched my father bury his wife in the partially frozen soil beneath the dead and dying trees. He did it with his bare hands, digging until the skin on his fingers peeled away, leaving behind meaty, blood-soaked nubs. When he was done, he stared past the tops of the trees and into the clouds overhead. His sigh was audible, even from so far away. I felt it on my skin, in the hairs on my arms, on the back of my neck. Though he wanted to mourn, there was no time. There was never any time. Night was approaching, and we weren't safe in the open – not at night. The night belonged to the *nasties*. Nothing was safe at night.

Kneeling at my side, father wrapped his arms around me and pulled me to his chest. His face was sweaty. The prickly beard on his chin rubbed against my scalp as I sobbed into the folds of his crinkly, cold jacket. He patted me gently on the back and allowed me to remain in his grasp for well over a minute. It was a minute longer than I expected.

"We have to go."

My legs had stopped working, so he lifted me. I couldn't stand. I couldn't do anything. When I tried to move, I fell. Father caught me. When my body refused to do anything other than stare at the mound of dirt beneath which mother was buried, he snatched me by the wrist and pulled me forward.

"We have to go, Megan."

They were the last words he'd speak for the remainder of the night and well into the morning.

We settled into an abandoned house just before nightfall. Father secured the doors as well as he could before coaxing me into a nearby closet, laying me down and covering me with his jacket. Gently, he slid the hair from my eyes, and for a while he just stared. I think he stopped breathing. For a fraction of a second, his mouth opened, dry lips parted to form a word. What emerged instead was a breathy nothingness that spoke volumes. There were no words, not any more. There never would be. After that, he was gone. The closet door closed and the darkness folded in. Father stood watch that night, the same as he had the night before and the one before that, as far back as I could recall.

My father was a good man. He wasn't a perfect man, but he was a good man. He loved me dearly, and he did his best to keep me safe. Despite the obstacles thrown his direction, he rarely faltered. Even when he faltered, he never gave up. He could have. It would have been easy. So many did.

I've met my fair share of men in the years since that specific night in that specific closet, listening to the *howlers* outside and shivering into the crumpled fabric of father's jacket. I've compared each and every one to him. His was the last generation born of a forgotten time. Once they were gone, there would be no one to remember the world as it once was—a time when the closet in which I hid served a different purpose entirely. Father was a relic of a place long since gone. He was a visitor in a world he could never truly understand, a passerby in the ugliness I called home.

In the morning, father made no mention of mother or what happened. He fastened the topmost button of my jacket, mussed my hair halfheartedly, and kissed me gently on the forehead.

He smeared the dirt from my cheek. "You're always so dirty."

He knew we had to keep moving. No matter what, we had to keep moving. Though my stomach was empty and the hunger pains stiff, I kept my discomfort to myself.

The journey was slow. The air was cold, colder than it had been in some time. A particularly harsh wind rattled the rusted exterior of the wagon we were dragging behind us, snaked between the trees and whistled an awful sound. Father pulled my hat down over my ears, lifted the hood of my jacket over my head, and tugged the strings tight.

"Are you okay?" His face was bright red, sweat frozen to his face. When the barely-there hints of sun hit it just right, it sparkled.

I remember liking that sparkle.

I wasn't sure how to respond. Every answer

seemed silly. I recalled my mother, the veins on her arms, and the look on her face. In her head, she was screaming. My mother died screaming.

"I'm fine."

It was a lie. It was a lie, and we both knew it.

It was the only answer I could give.

Midday, we came across a freshly mauled body in a ditch along the side of the road. Whoever it was, there wasn't much left – shredded bits of meat and shattered bone. Father shuffled across the street to investigate further. I planted my feet exactly where he instructed and didn't move. It was the *howlers*. It had to be the *howlers*. I didn't need to see the aftermath up close to recognize the work of the *howlers*. They rarely left anything behind. When they ate, they ate until they were full, until their bellies were so packed they could barely stand. What they couldn't finish they left behind with barely a thought. They weren't thinkers or packrats, and they certainly didn't plan ahead. They weren't capable of it. The *suckers* and the *gimps* were different animals entirely. The *suckers* were only after one thing, and the *gimps* were sloppy. The aftermath of a *gimp* feeding was the worst. Mother never let me see those. She'd cover my face with her hand and point my body in the opposite direction. One time I peeked through the cracks in her fingers and instantly wished I hadn't.

When father returned, he looked worried. His hand fell to my shoulder, fingers pinching the flesh beneath my jacket. After scanning the dried out trees on either side of the road, he moved his hand to the center of my back and nudged me forward. "We have to keep moving."

The remainder of the day was uneventful. Again night approached, and again we took shelter. Like every night prior, I found myself alone in the darkened closet of a rotted, weather-worn relic. Closets had become my bedrooms. I had so many of them. The *howlers* were quiet that night. I remember this specifically because it was rare. Maybe they were full from the night before. Maybe they simply didn't care.

Maybe we weren't worth it.

At the first hint of daylight, father fastened my topmost button, pulled my hat over my ears, lifted the hood over my head, and tied it beneath my chin. When he noticed my shoelace was undone, he dropped to one knee and secured it with a double knot. I told him I could have done it myself. This made him smile.

"Think we'll find it today?"

Father placed his hands behind his head, leaned back, and stretched the muscles in his back. "I don't know, sweetie. Maybe. I think we're close." He was looking through a tiny opening in a boarded window at the opposite end of the room, scratching at his beard. "We have to be close."

From his knapsack, he retrieved a single, unmarked can, set it on a nearby table and popped it open with his knife. "Found these last night. Little treat."

The contents were yellowish-orange, slimy, cut into tiny wedged shapes, and browning on the edges. I didn't know what it was, but it looked disgusting and old. It smelled even worse. Father dipped two fingers into the sticky glop and handed me a lump, which I immediately popped into my mouth. It was terrible. It was disgusting.

It tasted awful and delicious, and when I finished swallowing it, I extended my hand for another.

We were fairly early into the morning trek when we happened upon the compound. Father snatched me by my jacket, pulled me to the tree line, and told me to *get down*. At first I was confused. I couldn't understand what he was so worked up about. The compound didn't look too dissimilar from some of the buildings we'd come across over the years.

Father extended his finger through the browning bush we crouched behind, pointing to a grayish shed just inside the outer wall. "There. Look."

He was right. I didn't know how I'd missed it. Just beyond the rusted steel was a man in a dark jacket wearing a gasmask, a rifle tucked to his side. There was another man beside him and there seemed to be movement further back. These were the first *normals* we'd seen in months, and the first in years that didn't look destitute, or sick, or lost, or all of the above. Suddenly my heart was pounding. My fingers went to my mouth and my teeth to my nails.

"Is this it?"

Father didn't answer. He was scanning the compound, taking his time, trying to figure out exactly what he was seeing and what it meant. He stood for a moment, looking past the trees and further down the road, attempting to get a better feel for the layout of the structure. When I pulled at the fabric of his jacket, he pushed my hand away. When I tried to stand, he palmed the top of my head and shoved me to the dirt. After a few minutes of quiet examination, he dropped to one knee, placed his hands on my shoulders and turned me in his direction.

His eyes narrowed. "I need you to do exactly as I say, Megan. Do you understand?"

His hand moved from my shoulder, fingers

instead tapping lightly against the knife strapped to his thigh. "I need to make sure this is the place we were looking for." His hand returned to my shoulders for an instant before sliding up my neck and gently cupping my cheek. "And I need you to stay here while I do it."

My face scrunched. Suddenly my nose tickled, and the tickle shot into my eyes. My cheeks turned warm. My mouth opened, and my head shook. Father moved his other hand to my face and held it in place. "Don't shake your head at me. This isn't a request, young lady. You're going to do exactly as I say. Do you understand me?"
When my eyes began to water, he smeared it away with his thumbs.

"No matter what happens, I need you to stay right here. If I'm not back before the sun begins to set, I want you to make your way back to those houses we ran across an hour ago. Do you remember those houses?"

I didn't move.

"You go to the houses, you climb into a closet, and you stay there until I come get you. Do you understand?"

I couldn't answer. There was something in my throat, something massive, something so oversized it was keeping the words at bay. I didn't want him to leave. Why couldn't I go with him? The steel structure loomed over his shoulder, a great gray shadow of unknown possibilities. Why couldn't I go?

Father tightened his grip on my face, his thumbs constantly working to wipe the tears into my freezing cheeks. "You have to stop crying. I know it's hard, but you have to stop crying. You can't cry. Not in this place. Not ever. Crying is not allowed."

Instead of swallowing, I held my breath and thought of my mother, focusing my gaze on the deep-set wrinkles on father's forehead when looking into his eyes became impossible. There was a single gray hair mixed into one of his eyebrows. I hadn't noticed it until that very moment.

"Look at me, Megan."

I bit my quivering lip.

"If I'm not back by tomorrow night, you know what to do. You've done it enough times. You've done it before, and you can do it again. You're smart, and you're strong. You're stronger than you think."

He looked to the dirt, struggling to find the words. When he turned back, his expression had changed. The corner of his lip curled upward ever so slightly. "You look just like your mother."

Father pulled me to him, pressed his lips against my forehead as he had so many times before and held them there. I closed my eyes. I remember closing my eyes. I remember that I never wanted to open them again.

I'll never forget that moment, the wonderful sting.

When Father was done, he stood, pulled the knife from his side and handed it to me. He removed his backpack and dropped it to the dirt. "If I don't come back, you take all of this with you and head in another direction. Don't come after me and don't ever come this way again."

I almost followed him. It took everything I had not to follow him. I should have followed him.

I never saw him again.

2

I waited as long as I could, watching the compound, anticipating his return, counting shadows and seconds. When I got hungry, I ate. When I was done eating I waited some more. For hours I peeked through the twisted patch of bushes, careful to remain hidden while never taking my eyes from the compound. I waited as long as I could. A very real part of me believed I could somehow *will* him to return with the power of thought. It didn't work. When the sun began to set, I dropped father's backpack and knife into our wagon and headed for the abandoned houses as instructed. Once there, I found a closet and climbed inside.

It was especially cold that night. My bones shivered, toes went numb. For the first hour I cried into my shirt, biting down on the fabric to keep from making too much noise. The *howlers* were loud. They sounded close as if they were right outside, drooling, and huffing, and angry. At one point, there was a ruckus from another room; something rattled and broke. Nails dug into rotted wood, grinding it to splinters. Glass shattered. I swear I could hear one of them breathing, sniffing the air, trying desperately to latch onto the barely there scent of human flesh—my human flesh.

Or maybe I was imagining it.

Whatever the case, they didn't find me.

A few hours later it began to rain. The ceiling above me was hardly a ceiling at all. The roof of my hiding place had disappeared years ago. What remained was little more than jagged beams of broken wood and loose tiles. The rain seeped through the cracks with ease, dripping onto my head at a steady pace. In no time at all, I was sitting in at least an inch of water. I told myself it was only a matter of time before father found me; I whispered it into the damp fabric clinging to my chest. I imagined he would find me in the morning, kiss me on my forehead and tell me that the compound was *Homestead*. We'd share some of the food he'd brought back with him, practically a banquet. He'd tell me that we had finally found what we'd spent so many years searching for. I'd convinced myself this was exactly what would happen, and for some silly reason I actually believed it.

By morning I was soaked and freezing, my hair crunchy with ice. Father wasn't there. He hadn't found me, or kissed my forehead, or told me that we were done searching. None of that happened. It was still raining and I was still alone.

Most of the day was spent staring through the cracks of a boarded window facing the road. I saw nothing. The hours rolled on. The sun moved from one side of the sky to the other and dropped below the horizon. The moment it was gone I returned to my closet.

For three days I waited, hopeless, moving from the closet to the window and back to the closet again. It was longer than my father instructed and I didn't care. I couldn't just leave him. I had no idea where I would go. I wasn't as strong as Father believed or Mother had hoped. I wasn't very strong at all. At some point during my third night, cramped and shivering in the tiny closet, I stopped crying. I'm not sure why. The tears just dried up and went away. There weren't any left. My body shut down. I was sore and tired, lips cracked and throat raw. Swallowing was agony and the hunger pangs worse. Somehow, I managed to sleep. A quiet nothing settled in, gentle and weightless. *So quiet.* Father and Mother visited me in my dreams. Mother braided my hair into a tight ponytail to keep it off my neck. She zipped my jacket and wiped a smudge from my face. She gave me an extra helping of food and smiled so earnestly as I gobbled it up, despite her hunger. She kissed me on the cheek, her nose near my ear, warming breath against my face. When she sighed, she tilted her head slightly to the left. I giggled at her dimples. Father appeared over her shoulder, gazing down at me with a grin, the sun peeking through the clouds just over his head. It was all so beautiful. The clouds parted. I'd never seen the sun without the clouds. It was amazing.

Father brushed the hair from his eyes. "Look at this shit."

Mother's expression turned to stone. "Someone's here." She squeezed my shoulders, mouth open. Her teeth turned black, crumbling like ash and sliding down her throat. "Over there."

Father ripped me from her arms and lifted me into the air. He was terrified. He was disappointed. His grip was like iron and his fingers like *howler* teeth, ripping into my flesh. Behind him the sun began to crumple. It folded inward, cracked like glass, crinkled like burning paper. Father shook his head, mouthing something I couldn't hear. Suddenly he was moving backward. When I reached for him, I gripped only air. His face turned to dirt, caught a distant breeze and began to scatter. A billion points of sand disappeared into the darkness, swallowing him. His eyes had become the absence of everything. His nose exploded into barely-there shimmers of something unworldly. Before his mouth did the same, the sandy outline his lips had become mouthed a single word: "Run."

"Holy shit, it's a kid." Dirty hands ripped me from the safety of my closet. A crooked grin of yellow teeth greeted me when I opened my eyes. "It's a goddamn kid!"

He was tall and filthy, face coated in grime, hair wild and stiff. He lifted me into the air. I was weightless. I was helpless. I kicked my feet defiantly. Another set of hands snagged my legs and pulled them tight. Suddenly I was horizontal, squirming and clawing at anything within reach. When I tried to scream a hand covered my mouth.

Another voice from somewhere behind, gnarly like cracked glass: "Feisty one!"

Coarse fingers gripped my ankles. "Hold her legs! Get a hold on her goddamn legs!"

"Won't stop wiggling!"

"Hold her still, asshole!"

No matter what I did, no matter how hard I tried, I couldn't move. There were too many of them. The group of men surrounded me, laughing, a congealed lump of awful hands and arms foiling every attempt at escape. Out of sheer desperation, I bit one of the fingers covering my mouth. When he screamed, I smiled. I tasted blood. My face hit the floor, and the air left my lungs.

Everything went black.

When I woke, my legs were bound, arms tied behind my back, the ground bouncing beneath me. We were moving, driving. The interior of my lips tasted like dirt and metal, the aftertaste of blood. Tattered fabric soaked with the accumulated stains of *post war* hell was stuffed in my mouth and knotted at the rear of my head. Duffel bags crammed with scavenged goods boxed me like bookends. Just above me, a pair of legs. I followed them upward to a scruffy dark-haired man nursing a blood-soaked hand.

He noticed I was awake and smiled a terrifying smile. When he spoke, he growled. "How'ya doin', precious?"

When I cried, he chuckled.

It wasn't too long after that I recognized the familiar stone of the compound walls through the soot-coated window to my left. The walls seemed even larger up close, dark and dangerous, the jaws of some great beast. I thought of Father. They were taking me to Father. When the car came to a stop, a door behind me opened. Hands grabbed my ankles, pulled me into the light. A crowd had gathered, one grinning, twisted face after another, lined up like soldiers. A dark-skinned man with a scar running from the top of his head to the hem of his shirt tossed me over his shoulder. Gritty hands with filthy nails pawed at my body. The sunken face of a skeleton leaned in close and wiped the tears from my face, breathily whispering the world *pretty* while licking non-existent lips.

"What do you want me to do with her?" *Scarface* was talking to someone I couldn't see. When I tried to wiggle free, someone smacked me on the back of the head. Even after I'd stopped, they smacked me again. The group laughed.

"Dump her in the east wing. I'll let Travis know about her."

A few from the crowd followed along as *Scarface* carried me through the interior of the compound, rotted teeth clattering as they cackled. I opened my eyes in intervals, catching only the briefest glances of my surroundings, unable to get my bearings. There were small fires everywhere, pieces of unspecified meat roasting on spigots just above the flames. We passed a pile of bones, only half of which I recognized. A row of fifteen men crouched against a wall in the distance, thin and shivering, steel collars around their necks with chains attaching them. As we passed, a man at the rear of the chain lifted his head long enough to stare at me, eyes the color of rain, silver-blue and unblinking. He didn't look away. His eyes narrowed. His brow furrowed. Even as we moved from his line of sight, disappearing behind a row of tents, he never looked away. A moment later we approached a row of unassuming, poorly-made buildings, patched with pieces of scavenged steel. The inhuman screams from inside sent a shiver along my spine and into my legs. I'd heard similar screams before, *howlers,* lots of *howlers.* Whoever these people were, they were keeping *howlers* as pets.

We stopped at a small shed near the center of the compound. *Scarface* unlocked the door and tossed me inside. I landed on my knees, and then my head. The head hurt more. I rolled to my side, pulled my legs close to my chest, and buried my face in them. I couldn't stop crying. I wanted to stop crying. I needed to stop crying. Yet I couldn't stop crying.

Scarface kicked a cloud of sand in my direction. I inhaled it through my nose, into my lungs. My cried turned to coughs.

"Shut up."

The door slammed shut. The darkness folded in. Three locks clicked. I remember every one of them, so very simple and so very terrifying. They were the worst sounds I'd ever heard, cold and finite, the echoes of my mistakes. Though I tried my best to remove the idea from my head, I couldn't help but wonder if my father had heard them as well.

I'm not entirely sure how long I remained in that tiny room before I heard the locks again. It felt like hours. Could have been minutes. The air was stale, dank. It lingered on my lips, clung to my skin and stung my eyes. After the last of the three locks clicked, the door across from me opened. A tall man with short-trimmed hair stepped inside, dragging a chair. He face was clean-shaven, his hair neatly trimmed. He set the chair a few feet from my face, sat down, and crossed his legs. I'd never seen anyone cross their legs. He straightened his shirt, adjusted his collar. He looked fresh, cleaner than anyone I'd ever met, except for his boots. I remember his boots. His boots seemed massive, caked with bits of dirt and filth the color of blood. I closed my eyes and turned my head. His knuckles cracked.

It was at least a minute before he spoke. "Hello, little one." His voice was softer than I expected, almost inviting in a weird sort of way. "I just need to ask you a few questions. Won't take long, I promise. Think you're up for that?"

When I didn't respond, he nudged me with his boot. "Come on, sweetie. Don't make this any harder than it has to be. No one is going to hurt you."

I felt his hand on my head, long, skinny fingers gently brushing my hair, tucking it behind my ear the way mother would sometimes do. "Just a few quick questions and we'll get you out of here, okey dokey?"

My head nodded. I didn't want it to.

It didn't care.

Bloodboots dug his hands into my armpits, lifted and maneuvered me into a sitting position against a wooden crate. He cupped my chin and adjusted my head while using his thumb to wipe the dirt and tears from my eyes. "There you are. Much better. Little girls shouldn't be covered in dirt. It's not ladylike." Again he brushed the hair from my eyes. "What's your name, sweetie?"

My throat locked, lips quivered.

"Do you have a name? Would it help if I told you mine first?"

Again my stupid head nodded.

"I'm Travis. I'm sort of the man in charge around here." I felt his hand on my shoulder, fingers softly kneading my skin. "Do you have a name? I bet you have a name. Pretty girl like you, I bet you have a really pretty name."

"M-M-Me-Megan."

Stupid mouth. Even with my eyes closed, I could somehow sense he was smiling. I was giving him exactly what he wanted. My breath was slowing and my eyes drying, two more things I didn't want to happen, two more things I seemed to have no control over.

Bloodboots sat back in his chair and I heard it creak. He crossed his legs again and sighed. "Were you all alone out there, Megan? All by yourself?"

Father. I couldn't tell him about Father. I shouldn't tell him ab—"I was with my father."

Stupid.

For a moment it was quiet, so quiet I could hear *Bloodboots* swallow, so quiet I recognized the subtle sound of teeth grinding. "Just you and your pops, huh sweetie? Just the two of you alone against the world, huh? Hell, if that's the case, it's pretty remarkable you survived out there as long as you did. Goddamn amazing. Your daddy must be a heck of a guy, huh, a real survivor? Where is he, Megan? Where'd that amazing dad of yours run off to?"

My limbs locked. I bit my tongue. "I-I don't know." It wasn't a lie.

"It's okay, Megan. Take your time and think. How many people are with you and your daddy? It can't just be the two of you. That's silly. Do I look like the kind of guy who likes silly stories?"

"I-don't kno—"

"Yes you do, sweetie. Try real hard to remember." His voice was changing, half a whisper and half a growl, eerily monotone.

"I-I-I do-don—"

"Yes you do. You're not a little girl. You're old enough to count and smart enough to remember. No one is going to hurt you if you tell me what I want to know."

When I lowered my head again, *Bloodboots* returned it to its upright position. This time the act was more violent. It hurt my neck. "Who else is out there? Where are they and why did they leave you alone?"

My breath turned ragged. My chest heaved. Dry lips mouthed words devoid of substance or meaning. The next time he touched me, *Bloodboots* wasn't so sweet. He was done pretending. His fist snagged a handful of hair and jerked my head backward violently. Suddenly I could feel his breath on my face, inches away, spittle spraying my cheeks. When he stood from his chair, he dragged me with him, whipping me against a nearby wall and sending a jolt of pain across the whole of my back and into my legs.

"I have little patience for little girls, princess." His face moved again to mine. He was hunched over me, bent like a scarecrow, a malformed mess of jagged angles and coiled muscles. "As far as I'm concerned, you're only good for one thing, girly, and you're barely good for that yet."

His hands coiled into fists. "I'm going to ask you one more time. Before you respond, I want you to think very, very hard about what you're going to say. Double-check your work in that cute little head of yours. Ask yourself if it's the answer I want to hear before you spit it from your lips, because I won't ask again. There will be no more questions from this point on, Megan. To be perfectly honest, your answer won't change what's going to happen to you, nothing can. However, it might determine how badly it's going to hurt."

Outside, something exploded. Something else collapsed. Gunshots followed by a howl, then two more. *Bloodboots* let loose my hair as the door to the tiny shack swung open and *Scarface* stepped inside.

He removed a handgun from a holster on his hip. "We've got a problem, Travis. Goddamn *howlers* are loose."

3

Bloodboots shoved me to the floor. The back of my head hit the edge of a table and the front hit the dirt. He moved close to *Scarface*, teeth bared, hand already reaching for the gun strapped to his belt. "What? How?"

"Looks like someone snapped the locks on the stables. Bastards are loose all over the barracks."

Bloodboots kicked the wall beside him and the shelter wobbled. "Damn it!" Outside a *howler* roared. A gun fired. A man screamed, and then another. Things were getting louder by the second, coming in bunches, building to awful crescendo. *Bloodboots* looked at me just once before leaving, eyes wild and teeth bared. He readjusted the grip on his gun, brought it to his face, and glared at me over the barrel. For a moment I thought he was going to shoot me. A part even wanted him to.

He didn't.

Instead, he just stared, eyes narrowed, upper lip twitching. A noise emerged from his throat, an annoyed growl. With *Scarface* leading the way, he exited the room and charged into the fray. The door slammed shut, three locks clicked, and I was alone. I should have tried to wiggle free of my binds. There was a small window on the opposite end of the room—boarded up, but not very well. I could have pried those boards loose and created an opening just large enough for me to slide through. Once outside, I could have run. I could have kept running until my legs gave way and I couldn't run anymore. I could have at least lifted myself off the floor.

I didn't.

Instead, I did nothing at all. I cried into the floor. I closed my eyes and mashed my face into the wood and filth. I thought of mother, the look on her face that day on the side of the road, the last time I saw her. Even though we were with her, father beside her with his fingers in her hair and his lips on her cheek, she was alone. Whatever she was going through in that moment, belonged only to her. Whatever she was seeing, only she could see. My mother died alone. Maybe we all die alone. Maybe there's no other way.

In the midst of the noise outside, I heard the locks again, three of them in close succession. I didn't know if it was *Scarface* or *Bloodboots* or any of the greasy, disgusting men that pawed me when I was carried into the compound. I told myself it didn't matter. Whoever they were, they weren't done with me. This was only the beginning. It was going to hurt. *Bloodboots* said it would hurt. I closed my eyes and prepared for the worst.

The door swung open. A hand grabbed my forearm, lifted me into the air. "Get up." The voice wasn't familiar. I didn't recognize it and I didn't care to. It wasn't *Scarface* and it wasn't *Bloodboots*. It wasn't Father or Mother. It didn't matter.

"Damn it, kid!"

He was hurried, impatient. "Don't have time for this."

Whoever he was, I was suddenly on his shoulder, bouncing as we sped through a warzone. Something hit the ground behind us, a mound of dirt tossed fifteen feet into the air and another after that. Gunshots came in multiples, spitting in bursts, destroying everything, whizzing past my face. Something collapsed. Rusted steel bent and old wood snapped. Somewhere behind me, something exploded. Then another, this time much closer. In every direction there was madness. My ears were ringing, my face covered in a layer of soot. Through tear-soaked eyes, I watched a massive creature, fifteen feet tall and engulfed in flames, slam into the side of jeep. The gargantuan beast lifted half the vehicle off the ground, nearly tipping it over. I could smell its hair burning, hear the agony in its screams. The smell was beyond words. I'd never encountered anything like that smell. When it opened its fiery mouth to roar, a spatter of bullets tore into its back, rippling up its spine and transforming flesh into tattered meat. Something else exploded nearby. I could feel it reverberate in my skull. Thinking my ears were bleeding, I covered them with my hands and pressed tight. We passed a man curled up in the dirt, blood-soaked fingers dug into the flesh of his face, half his head engulfed in crackling orange and red. Even when I closed my eyes I could see him, an impossible silhouette of black on black, a wild burst of sound against a wall of nothing.

Shortly after, the insanity began to fade. I didn't know where we were or where we were headed, but we were getting further away with every step. I bounced atop my savior's shoulder for nearly ten minutes, the smell of sulfur and scorched fur evaporating into the night. Twigs snapped under the weight of boots. A branch tangled itself in my hair, broke from its tree and bounced along with us. Keeping my hands on my ears, I opened my eyes. The walls of the compound were gone, replaced by the dried out darkness of the forest. The man carrying me stopped, breath ragged, chest heaving. He leaned forward and I slid off his shoulder into the dirt and onto my rear.

That's when I recognized his face: *eyes the color of rain, silver-blue and unblinking.* It was the man from the courtyard, the one with the light hair, the one who stared at me and refused to look away.

"Can you run?" His voice was like charcoal, like clanking stones. When I didn't answer he asked again, emphasizing every word. "Can. You. Run?"

I nodded.

"Then do it." With one hand he lifted me to my feet. "Follow me. Stay close and you stay alive."

I did.

For at least an hour, we moved through the forest, faint whispers of moonlight our only guide. He was hurried but cautious, careful with every step. I'm not sure why I kept so close to him, gripping the fabric of his shirt with one hand and tucking myself into his side. I probably shouldn't have followed so blindly. In hindsight, I suppose it was a silly thing to do.

I was becoming quite good at silly things.

Truthfully, I didn't know what else to do or where to go. My surroundings were a dead maze of shredded bark and fog. Nothing seemed familiar and everything seemed the same. Father had rarely let me drift from the safety of the road, especially not at night and certainly never so deep into the forest. The forest belonged to the *nasties* and the night was when they fed. The forest wasn't safe.

Half an hour into the trip, my legs were sore, knees on fire, every step like trudging through broken glass. When I tried to take a break, my traveling companion snatched me by the arm. "Can't stop. Not yet."

When I started to cry, he told me to *stop*. When I tried to ask him a question, he told me bluntly to *shut up*. When I eventually crumpled to the ground, unable to go any farther, he forced me back to my feet. "Can't stop, kid."

The moon was directly overhead when we came upon a small shack in the woods, old, barely holding together. A substantial breeze could have toppled it, a single *howler* would have reduced it to splinters. The moment we were inside, I looked for a closet. When I found one, I crawled inside and closed the door behind.

It opened a moment later. "What the hell are you doing?" My blue-eyed companion was still staring at me, wide-eyed, confused. His eyes never moved. His expression never changed. I wasn't sure he knew how to blink. "I need you to watch the back door."

"Wha...? I-I don—don—"

He snatched me by the wrist, dragged me into the open. "Going to be a long night. We're in the middle of the forest, exposed here. Sleeping won't work. No time for sleep."

"B-but I-I don't know..." I wasn't sure what he was suggesting. I needed to be in the closet. It was dark, we were in the middle of the forest, and I felt naked without the closet. The closet was safe.

He kneeled down, putting us on the same level. My teeth clattered, dry eyes aching to produce tears. His hands grabbed hold of my biceps, pressed them to my torso, and squeezed. For a moment, the shivering stopped.

He motioned to a partially boarded window on the opposite end of the tiny enclosure. "Stay by the window near the back. That's all you have to do. Just keep your eyes open. If you see anything, you come to me. I'm right over there, right at the window beside the door. I'm not going anywhere. Can you do that?"

I nodded.

It was a lie.

My new friend nodded back. He retrieved a knife from his belt, placed it in my hand, and wrapped my fingers around the handle before nudging me in the direction of the window. The steel weapon felt massive, cold, and heavy, stained with flakes of dirt, blood, and unspecified filth. As I approached my post, I reminded myself to breathe. I felt dizzy. Every step was a struggle, inhaling an exercise. Through the cracks in the wood haphazardly nailed to the window frame, I watched the forest, gazing through the black and the trees, listening to my heart pound, sweaty hands struggling to hold my weapon. I'll never forget that night. For as long as I live, I'll never forget that night. Though my blue-eyed savior was just twenty feet away, it might as well have been miles. For the first time in my life I was alone, really alone. For the first time in my life, my safety was my own. Every breeze held the promise of disaster, every falling leaf the end of days. The forest became a living thing, angry and hungry, ugly-mouthed, a monster with its full attention settled squarely on me.

Wherever I was, there was no going back. Whatever happened was going to happen. There was no stopping it. I no longer had a say. When something deep in the belly of the shadows moaned, howled and announced its presence to any and all. I gripped the knife in my hand so tight that my knuckles turned white.

I was already becoming whoever I was destined to become.

4

It was dawn when my new *friend* informed me we needed to leave. "They had too much on their plates to deal with putting a search party on us last night...different story this morning. We need to move."

I'd surprised myself the night before. I managed to stay awake until the morning. It took so long for the day to arrive. Minutes felt like hours, hours like days, the dark forest unrelenting and the sun a tardy visitor. My eyes were heavy. My arms were sore, legs weak, fingers shivering around the handle of the knife, frozen sweat clinging to my forehead. I thought

I would die; all night long, I honestly believed it. It was a fact. It was simply a matter of time. And yet, despite my fears, nothing attacked. The forest groaned and screamed, but never made good on the threats. When my head began to dip from exhaustion, I glanced in the direction of my bearded companion. He didn't move, not once, a stoic silhouette against the moonlight from the window, cut from stone and tethered to the floor, an unyielding protector. I suppose, in some ways, he terrified me more than anything lurking outside.

Not long after the sun rose, we were again trudging through the woods, moving farther from the compound with every step, farther from Father. I wanted to say something, tried on more than one occasion. When I opened my mouth, nothing emerged, second thoughts and regrets too prevalent to overcome. Instead, I kept my mouth shut and my head down. I followed.

Around midday we emerged from the trees and came across a stretch of road. I'd never been so happy to see the road. It felt familiar, felt like home. When night approached, we took refuge in a shattered husk of a house deep in the belly of a hundred others exactly the same. I'd stayed in similar places for the whole of my life, shells of a past I only vaguely remembered, forgotten memories of a world I'd never know.

My parents rarely talked about their life before *the end*, before I was born. On the rare occasions they did, it was with a heavy heart. They wanted to forget the past. That much was obvious. Reliving it, even momentarily and even in their heads, made that impossible. I was born in the aftermath of whatever happened, whatever transformed the world to cinder and ash. I was a product of this place. Its dust and its monsters were mine. It was all I knew, all I'd ever know.

My dreams had always been nightmares.

That night *Blueeyes* let me sleep, not that he had any choice in the matter. I was done for. My eyes refused to stay open. I couldn't lift my arms. He told me it was *okay*. He claimed we were safe among the ruins outside the forest, safer from *howlers* anyway. The *gimps* were another story entirely. *Gimps* seemed to love the ruins, plodding aimlessly from broken building to collapsing husk, limp-necked and dead-eyed. I'd only seen a few of them up close at that point in my life, sunken faces of rotted flesh, eyes like filthy water, cloudy and not quite there. The *gimps* were slow. When they weren't in packs, they were mostly easy to escape, and when they were in packs, you could smell them coming a mile away.

I slept in the open, a closet just a few feet away. *Blueeyes* told me I should keep close, that the closet would only make things harder if we needed to leave in a hurry. I *suppose* it made sense.

In the morning I found him staring out the window, knife in one hand, expression as steady as ever. I don't think he slept. As far as I knew, he never had. It took me a while to work up the courage to tell him I was hungry. He fed me immediately, cracking open a can of something he'd discovered in the ruins overnight. It tasted awful. Everything always tasted awful.

I didn't let him know what I thought of it.

Instead, we sat in silence looking at the floor, staring at the walls, looking everywhere but at each other. In a strange way, he seemed as scared of me as I was of him. Nibbling at the pile of greenish-yellow glop, I would steal momentary glances, watching him through the spaces in my dangling hair. He moved from the windows to the doors, pacing back and forth, occasionally leaning his head outside to scan the exterior. He wasn't a huge man; larger than my father, but not a mountain like *Scarface* or as tall as the *Bloodboots*. Even then, I noticed the hint of sadness in his eyes. He tried his best to hide it and mostly succeeded, but I noticed. I was good at noticing things, even then, details others missed. Father once told me it was my *gift*.

Blueeyes was sad. He was hurting. It was subtle, just below the surface, painted into the wrinkles on his forehead and the lines beneath his eyes. Father had the sadness too. And mother. *They all did.* When *Blueeyes* removed his jacket, I saw the scars for the first time, so many scars. They covered his arms, long and short, dark and light, like cracks in the pavement, crumbled stone, eventually disappearing beneath the sleeve of his shirt and the hem of his collar. Some of them resembled bite marks, but I knew that was impossible. When he noticed me staring, I looked away.

When I was done eating, he told me we had to keep moving, said something about another, much safer housing development further down the road. He mentioned seeing *gimp* tracks on the next block over, told me it was only a matter of time before they forgot where they were headed in the first place and circled back in search of something familiar.

I wasn't crazy about the idea. I let him know. "We have to go back to the compound."

I don't know why I said it. It spit from my lips without hesitation or warning. Once it was out, there was no putting it back.

"What?" He was eyeing me from across the room, hands at his sides, eyes narrowed and mouth hanging open.

"W-we have…" I couldn't blink. I couldn't

breathe. When my lower lip started to quiver, I bit it, turned away. I couldn't look at him and say what I needed to say. Looking at him was impossible. "M-my fath-father. We have to go back. My father…my f-father is in there, in the compound. We have to go back."

There was no hesitation in his response. "We're not going back."

Nor was there in mine. "We have to go back."

Why wouldn't I shut up? *I needed to shut up.* I kept saying things I knew I shouldn't say, things he didn't want to hear. I closed my eyes and lowered my head, trying to control my breathing, half expecting to feel his knife in my back. I still couldn't turn around. If I'd turned around, I never would have said what I needed to say.

Again there was a pause. He sighed before he finally spoke. I remember the sigh. The sigh might as well have been a scream. "Your father is dead."

A knife in the back would have been less painful. Tiny hands coiled into tiny fists so tight my fingernails dug into the flesh of my palms. My jaw tightened, chest heaved, and nostrils flared. I spun around, charged at him with my head lowered and arms raised. "Shut up! Shut up! You don't know anything! You don't know!"

I slammed into him at full speed, collided with his chest, arms swinging, teeth bared, screaming at the top of my lungs. "You don't know anything! I don't know you! You don't know my father and I don't know you!" When he caught my fists, I kicked his legs. When he trapped my legs, I swung my fists. When I couldn't use either, I gave him a head butt to the chest. He shoved me backward, pinning me against a nearby wall. I bit his arm.

"Stop it! Damn it, stop it!"

I was like a tornado, an eighty-pound bundle of pent-up rage and exposed nerves. Every time he thought he had me under control, I wiggled loose. The moment my fists were free, I punched. I hammered his chest and his neck, kicked him in the shins and kneed him in the groin. I didn't care. He didn't have any right to say what he said, even less of a right to say it the way he'd said it. None of it made sense anyway. Why was he helping me? Why did he care? Who was he? *He was no one. He was nothing,* a liar. I wanted him to take it back. I wanted him to go away. I never wanted to see his stupid face or his ugly blue eyes again! I didn't want to be in that broken down house with him, and I regretted accepting his food. I wanted to be back on the road with Mother and Father. I wanted my closet back. I hated him. In that moment, I hated him more than I'd hated anything.

When the glass in the partially boarded window on the opposite end of the room unexpectedly shattered, I stopped screaming, he stopped holding—everything stopped.

Blueeyes immediately retrieved the knife from his belt and growled under his breath. "Shit."

A rotted arm snapped through the newly broken glass, twisted fingers pawing at the air. A head of sunken cavities and peeling flesh leaned into the room. A *gimp*. The creature sniffed the air like a dog searching for a scent. Its milky eyes settled in our direction, its mouth opened, rotting teeth clinging to nonexistent gums, upper lip quivering. The moment it realized what it was looking at, it screamed. I'd never heard one of them scream—so human, and yet so *not*. The wall beside the window shook and the head of another *gimp* leaned in. Something slammed into the back door, knocking loose rusted hinges. The window across from us exploded inward, tossing shards of glass onto my feet. They were all around us. We were surrounded.

Blueeyes snatched me by the wrist, nearly pulling my arm from the socket, dragging me toward the stairs. " Move! Now!"

It happened so quickly. In a matter of seconds the room was packed with *gimps,* mindlessly jockeying for position, shoving and screaming, moaning like injured animals. It was awful, a sea of filth and madness. At least ten pairs of distant eyes locked onto us as we hustled upstairs, aged wood cracking with every step. Jaws snapped at air, limbs like twisted wire flailing in every direction. *Blueeyes* pulled me into the first open doorway, slammed the door behind him, and wedged his back against it. The room was small, littered with bits of debris, a broken bed and leftover junk from what used to be a desk wedged in the corner. The windows were boarded tight.

There was no way out.

The weight of the *gimp* horde pounded against the door, knocking *Blueeyes* forward before he dropped his shoulder and slammed his full weight against it once again. I could hear their fingers, so many fingers clawing at the wood, peeling paint and tearing scraps of their own flesh in the process.

The monsters were filling the area outside the room, packed tight and getting tighter, beating against the single piece of wood separating them from their meal. *Blueeyes* was struggling to keep it closed. The next time it opened, a *gimp* hand found its way inside, snatched his shirt. Without hesitation, he swung his knife upward, through the decayed forearm of the creature, snapping rotted bone and spraying blood across the floor.

With his free hand, he pointed across the room.

"The window! Pry those boards from the window!"

I tried. I really did try. I wrapped my fingers around the wood and pulled. I put my foot on the wall and used it for leverage. I hit them with my shoulder and punched them with my hands. When none of that worked, I wiped the tears from my face and tried it all again. They wouldn't budge. No matter what I did or how hard I did it, they wouldn't move. The moaning was getting louder. Wood cracked, splinters sprayed. Two dead fingers wormed their way through a crack and peeled a bit of the door away. They were tearing it apart. *Blueeyes* slipped, and fell, and landed on his rear, struggling to keep the creatures at bay. It was only a matter of time. One of their heads smashed into the partially open door and bit down. Bloody teeth popped from its mouth. *Blueeyes* put his knife in the space between its eyes. The creature's decayed skull folded inward, pus and chunks of meat squishing from inside. I turned my head, dropped to my knees, closed my eyes, and put my hands over my ears. I couldn't listen anymore. It was too much. It was happening too fast.

Blueeyes screamed at me. "The closet!" I barely heard him over the noise. He screamed again. "Damn it! Look at me!"

When I finally looked up, he was on his knees, shoulder pressed to the door, boots sliding against the wooden floor. At least ten *gimp* arms twitched like spider legs at the joint. One of them was pulling at his jacket while another had a handful of his hair. Stabbing at the wiggling appendages, face peppered with blood, *Blueeyes* pointed at a door on the far end of the room. "The closet! Get in the closet and close the door! Do not come out until I tell you!"

I moved without hesitation, so fast I tripped. Instead of trying to stand, I crawled. All I could see was the closet. I'd never moved so fast in my life, and never with such purpose. In that moment, I didn't care about *Blueeyes*. I didn't care that I was leaving him to face a horde of *gimps*. I didn't care if he lived or died. I didn't care about anything. When I reached the closet door, I opened it, slid inside and pressed myself against the back wall.

It was black in there, pitch black.

Outside my little black safe haven, things were anything but safe. Wood tore and splintered. Something crashed. *Blueeyes* screamed. He wasn't hurt, wasn't in pain. It wasn't that kind of scream. It was more like a battle cry, an angry wail. Feet trampled into the room, so many of them, all at once. A body hit the floor. Another hit the wall. Something collapsed. Glass shattered. The floor was shaking, walls creaking. Coat hangers flopped loose from the bar above me, raining down onto my head. In no time at all, the groans became louder, more vicious. The voice of *Blueeyes* melded into the fold, intermixed with everything awful until it was one and the same. I'm not sure how long I sat in that closet with my knees to my chest, shivering, biting my arm to keep from screaming. It felt like forever.

Eventually, it all stopped. Everything always stops.

When it was quiet again, I pulled my arm from my mouth. I had bitten down so hard that I'd drawn blood. Believe it or not, until that very moment, I'd never seen my own blood.

"Come on out."

It took me a full minute after hearing his voice to crack the closet door and peek out; even then, I barely worked up the nerve. *Blueeyes* was in the center of the room, head down, hands and arms covered in blood, face turned crimson. Around him were *gimp* corpses—so many corpses. Their bodies were like fallen branches, jumbled, unnatural things bent in unnatural ways. Less than a foot away from the closet the severed head of one of the creatures wobbled unevenly, dead eyes swaying back and forth in a pool of blood, staring right at me. *Blueeyes* lifted the hem of his shirt, wrapped it around the hand holding his knife, and used it to wipe away the blood. He didn't look at me, not once.

He pulled the hood over his head. "Not safe here. Have to keep moving."

Megan

When he held out his hand, I took it.

5

The trip to the new housing development was quiet. Trips were always quiet with *Blueeyes,* but this was a different sort of quiet, quieter than quiet. After a bit of searching, he found a *relatively secure* house where we found a *relatively secure* room and settled in for the night. *Blueeyes* told me to sleep, said it was best, claimed I needed to be fresh for the next day. I couldn't sleep. I tried to sleep, but I couldn't. There were minutes here and there where I approached something vaguely resembling sleep. I waded in and out of consciousness, curled into a fetal position, listening to the *howlers* in the distance. Mostly, I watched my traveling companion, peeking through half-closed eyes, unsure of what to make of him. The way he'd killed those *gimps*... I didn't think it was possible. It shouldn't have been possible. In spite of my unease, I felt safe around him. I couldn't explain it. I guess it didn't make much sense. For a while, he cleaned his knife, fingernails chipping dried blood, using his shirt to dust away what remained. When he finished cleaning, he stood at the window, just staring. Every time a *howler* moaned, his muscles tensed. Even when he was relaxed, he was never really *relaxed*. He was coiled, twitchy, always ready to strike, ready for anything. When he was finished staring, he moved to the corner of the room, dropped to his rear, and pulled his legs to his chest. For a long time he didn't move. He didn't scratch his beard, or stretch his legs, or mumble. He barely breathed. He just sat.

Briefly he closed his eyes.

"Go to sleep."

No, he wasn't sleeping. He caught me peeking.

"I-I can't." It wasn't a lie. "The noises...I-I can't...the noise, it bothers me."

He sighed, shook his head just enough for me to notice. "Would have thought you'd be used to that by now." He glanced up briefly, his face hidden in shadow. "We have a long way to go tomorrow, can't stop. If we don't keep moving they'll catch up to us. If they catch up to us...forget it."

I sat up, crossed my legs, brushed the hair from my eyes, and pinned it behind my ear. I didn't want to sleep. Sleeping was pointless. *Blueeyes* never slept. "Why are they after us?"

He shook his head again, then paused, fingers twiddling at the hole in the leg of his pants. He almost seemed nervous when he spoke to me, at least as nervous as he could be. "They're not after *us*, they're after me."

"Why?"

"Because."

"Because why?"

"You ask too many questions."

"Is it because you let the *howlers* loose at the compound?"

"That didn't help."

"Because you stole me?"

"Probably."

"Is that all?"

"No."

"What else?"

"Nothing else. Go to sleep."

"I can't."

"Yes you can."

"I tried."

"Try harder."

He didn't seem so nervous anymore; he seemed annoyed. I should have stopped, left it at that. I should have closed my eyes and gone to sleep. I didn't. "What else?"

"Because of your father."

Once again he'd managed to shut me up. I stopped asking questions, stopped breathing. My chest tightened, throat locked, mouth dry.

Blueeyes looked at me. His expression seemed familiar, the same as that first time I saw him in the compound. "Your father...I was there, in the compound, when he came knocking."

Suddenly I was the one unable to blink.

Once he started, he didn't stop. That was his way. He never spoke unless prodded. He also never wasted his words. "I'd only been there a week, maybe two. A week more and I would have been dinner. I let my guard down, got caught. Stupid. Wasn't paying attention. I'm not sure what he said to piss them off, your father, but he said something. Or not, I don't know. Maybe Travis was just having a bad day. Whatever he did, it rubbed that asshole the wrong way. Your old man tried to reason with them, tried his damndest…didn't matter."

I didn't want him to continue, but I started him down this road. It was my fault. He almost never talked. I forced him to talk and he was talking, and he wouldn't shut up. His brow narrowed, lips tightened. Once he was looking right at me, refusing to look away.

"You don't need to know the details…wouldn't serve a purpose. Your father seemed like a good man, I guess, the sort of man who believed there were others like him left in the world. There aren't. Nothing left but monsters anymore." He paused. "Maybe that's all there ever were."

The first time I tried to speak, I choked. The second time, I choked again. "Y-you, you saw m-my father?"

Blueeyes didn't nod. He didn't need to.

"Did he say—? Did you talk? I mean…d-did he say anything?"

"He said your name. Megan."

My face cracked, body crumbled. My head fell to my hands and my eyes began to water.

"He said your name, and he said he was sorry."

6

When morning came I found myself a bit of food, fastened the topmost button on my jacket, and pulled the hood tight over my head. While I'd cried for Father the night before, I hadn't cried for long. He wouldn't have wanted me to. He was gone. I loved him the same as I loved Mother, but they were both gone and they were never coming back. Nothing would change that. Especially not tears.

It was cold that day, so cold I could see my breath. The sky looked different, darker. The clouds were heavy, packed and full, bottoms of dark obsidian. Despite their size, they remained slaves to the wind. They went where it told them to, as quick as it desired. Occasionally, they would roar, angry threats of impending eruption, frustrated with the order of things.

I followed closely behind *Blueeyes*. We stuck to the road and made good time. There was no chatter when we traveled, no wasted energy or movement. Every step was calculated. Every moment served a purpose. When we found something we thought could be useful, we kept it. When we stumbled across something that served no purpose, we ignored it. Everything was by the book, without deviation. In a world where nothing was predictable, everything was predictable. *Blueeyes* wouldn't have had it any other way.

A few hours into the journey we happened on the leftovers of a *howler* attack. It was impossible to tell exactly how many people had been murdered, devoured. Bits of shredded flesh and fabric clung loosely to crumpled bones and flapped in the breeze. The bodies were torn apart, mauled and licked clean. Slick pools of frozen blood stained the pavement, sprayed in every direction, glistening in the hint of sunlight able to sneak through the clouds. It smelled awful.

Everything always smelled.

At that point in my life I'd never seen a kill so fresh. Whatever happened must have happened the night before. While I was crying, they were dying.

While I was mourning the things I'd lost, these people were losing everything. When I looked away, *Blueeyes* grabbed me by the arm, pulled me closer. He said I should see the kill up close, told me I needed to realize what I was dealing with. From less than a foot away, I looked down on the remains of something that could have been a man or a woman—there was no way of knowing. There was no face to speak of, only skull and crystallized blood, bits of brain. There was someone else lying beside the corpse, a few more piles of half-frozen meat and cartilage a bit further down the road. Everything recognizably human about them had been consumed. The *howlers* took it all. They had eaten everything, erased the entire group from existence. Ribs were demolished, arms broken in two, chests ripped open and insides scooped out. I saw something I thought might have been a spine. I also saw the pavement underneath.

Blueeyes nudged the remains with his boot and shook his head. "They won't leave anything. You need to be aware of that." He looked down at me, face as stern as ever. "You can't talk to them. You can't reason with them. They don't know what you're saying. Even if they did, they wouldn't care. They don't care how old you are. They don't care that you're a girl. They don't care that you've never shot a gun or don't have any weapons. You're just food. That's all that matters. If you cry, you're easy food. Do you understand?"

I nodded.

For the first time since we'd met, I *think* he believed me.

When everything that needed to be said was said, we scavenged what we could from the scattered remains of their backpacks and moved on.

"We have to keep moving." That's what *Blueeyes* said. "We can't stop moving."

It was a few hours later that we heard the screams, a woman and a man and someone else, further down the road and out of sight. *Blueeyes* picked me up, ran off the road, and dove into the trees. We dropped to the dirt behind a lump of dead grass and fallen leaves.

His hand went to my mouth, index finger to my lips. *"Shhh."*

A few seconds later we heard engines, two of them. Through a pile of dead branches I watched as a truck pulled into view. It was filthy, the exterior covered in dents, paint chipping, windows coated in a layer of soot. Haphazardly built onto the back of the wheezing, steel beast was a cage. Inside the cage were people. A dark-haired man with a graying beard that hung to his belt beat on the bars, pulling and punching, screaming while struggling to keep his balance. Behind him a woman cradled two children, their heads buried in her chest, skinny arms crisscrossed at her waist. I couldn't see their faces, couldn't tell if they were boys or girls. Whatever they were, they were scared. The woman's fingers spread across the backs of their heads, intertwined with masses of matted hair. When the truck came to a sudden stop, the screaming man stumbled, fell forward, awkwardly landed on his face. When he popped up again, his nose was bleeding, crimson staining the whiskers below his nose. A second vehicle pulled behind the first. It was larger, louder, reinforced with pieces of scavenged metal, tires wrapped in chain. When it stopped, a mass of black smoke belched from the rear. The engine popped and I jumped. *Blueeyes* wrapped his arms around me, held me still and put his hand over my mouth.

I jumped again when the driver door opened. *Scarface* stepped out.

I never wanted to see him again. A part of me actually believed I wouldn't.

Wishful thinking.

The man in the cage kicked the bars and tried to wedge his head in the space between, barking like a trapped animal. "You son of a bitch! You can't do this! I have a family! You can't do this! This isn't the way it's supposed to be! We shouldn't be living like this!" When *Scarface* was close enough, the bearded man lunged forward, tried to snag his shirt.

It didn't work.

Scarface caught his arm, pinned it back against the cage, and used the crowbar in his freehand to smash the back of the man's hand. His wife screamed something unintelligible, smothered her children to her chest. Her hands went to their ears in a desperate attempt to keep them from hearing their father scream. Every time the crowbar connected with bone, the bearded man roared. Every time he roared, *Scarface* hit him harder. When *Scarface* finally released him from his grip, the man's hand was a mauled mess of meat, blood, and pulverized bone. He stumbled back, hand at his chest, cradling the demolished appendage.

Scarface tapped the cage with the crowbar. When he spoke, his voice was measured, calm. "Stop screaming." I think I saw him smile.

The bearded man didn't stop.

Scarface repeated himself. "Shut up."

Instead of stopping, the screaming got louder.

The window on the truck rolled down, a head popped out, a toothless mouth barked. "We can't have him screaming like that! *Howlers* will hear that shit from miles away! Shut that son of a bitch up!"

Scarface wacked the bars again, this time with a bit more force. "Shut up! You better shut the fuck up right now, old man! This is your last warning!"

I'm not sure if the bearded man didn't hear him, didn't care, or was unable to stop. In the end I suppose it didn't matter. His wife let go of her children, tugged at his shirt, begging him to stop. He didn't listen. He wouldn't listen. What happened next happened quickly. *Scarface* retrieved a gun from the holster on his hip, pointed it at the bearded man and fired. His chest exploded. A mass of crinkly gray hair parted and a spray of blood shot forth. The bearded man crumpled like paper, body went limp, legs turned to rubber. He collapsed, folded, hunched forward and rolled to his side. With a single gunshot, it was over.

Just like that, he was gone.

I'd never seen anyone die. I'd seen an awful lot in my years, but I'd never seen someone die, not like that, not murdered, not so close. My body reacted independent of my brain. It did exactly what I didn't want it to do, exactly what *Blueeyes* was hoping to avoid. I bit down on my traveling companion's hand, tasted blood. Suddenly I was standing. Suddenly I was screaming. It was stupid. It was childish. Mother would have been disappointed; father would have shaken his head. *Blueeyes* tried to pull me back down, tried to minimize the damage. It was too little. It was too late. *Scarface* turned, looked right at me. Our eyes met.

So stupid.

Before I knew what was happening, *Blueeyes* scooped me up, pulled me to his side, and ran. I was like baggage in his arms, useless baggage, dead weight bobbing wildly, limbs flailing as we hurried into the forest. *Scarface* screamed something; someone responded with a louder scream. A bullet whizzed past my head, hit the bark of a tree beside me, shot splinters into my hair. Another pelted the dirt at *Blueeyes'* feet, threw it back in my face. Within seconds they were all around us, hitting everything, a violent rain of steel laying waste to the forest. One of them tore through *Blueeyes'* shoulder. He jerked forward, nearly losing his grip on me. Despite the injury, he never stopped moving, or ducking, or jumping. *Blueeyes* moved with incredible precision, as if he'd lived in the forest his entire life, knew every fallen tree or oversized rock. Yet, no matter how fast he ran, I still heard the voices, heard *Scarface*. He was following us. He wasn't giving up. When we came upon an old brick wall, *Blueeyes* hopped over it. He ducked into an abandoned cabin, hustled through a living room and a kitchen, and out the back door. We passed a shed, then returned to the thick of the forest. The gunshots began to disappear. The voices faded away. *Blueeyes* kept moving, over a small hill and down the other side, sliding, struggling to remain on his feet, to keep from letting me slip from his arms. It wasn't until we reached a cliff that he stopped. There was nowhere left to run.

Still dangling from his side, I gazed over the edge of the gargantuan ravine impeding our progress. It was massive, at least two hundred feet of jagged rock leading nowhere but down, a barely noticeable river at the bottom. Climbing was impossible, heading back into the forest even more so.

Blueeyes lowered me to the ground. "Shit." We were trapped.

"Dead end, asshole." *Scarface* stepped from the trees, massive chest heaving, struggling to catch his breath, gun in hand.

The sound of his voice stabbed me in the chest, sent a chill across my body and into my legs. *Blueeyes* turned to face him. He placed his hand on my shoulder, slowly maneuvered me behind him, transforming himself into a human shield. His fingers coiled into fists, cold knuckles cracked.

Again *Scarface* smiled. "Heh."

His eyes moved from me to *Blueeyes* and his smile disappeared. He readjusted the grip on his gun. "Travis has been looking for you two since the *howler* incident…sort of obsessed. He wants you alive. Personally, I don't give a shit. Either way, you're coming with me."

When *Blueeyes* spoke, he growled. "Not going anywhere."

Scarface lifted his gun and pointed it in our direction. Steel clicked. "Wasn't giving you an option, Hoss."

In a single movement, *Blueeyes* retrieved his knife, dropped his shoulders, and barreled forward. The gun fired. A bullet tore through his arm, sent his knife flying. I dropped to the grass, covered my head. Before *Scarface* could get off another round their bodies collided, meshed into a grunting, snarling heap of violence. They hit the ground, bounced off a rock and rolled. *Scarface* yelled. *Blueeyes* snarled. A cloud of dirt engulfed them. *Blueeyes* punched and *Scarface* punched back. The moment *Blueeyes* was on top, he dropped his elbow to *Scarface's* nose. Bone shattered, cartilage turned to dust. A fountain of blood spewed forward. When *Scarface* was on top, he kneed *Blueeyes* in the groin, butted him with his bloody forehead, tried to stick his thumb in his eye. His fingers went to *Blueeyes'* mouth, ripping at his cheek, pinning his head to the dirt. In the distance I heard voices, lots of voices getting closer. *Blueeyes* heard them too. Somehow he reversed position, ended up on *Scarface's* chest. He had the advantage. There wasn't much time. He didn't hesitate.

He never hesitated.

One after another, his fists pummeled *Scarface's* head until they were soaked in blood, until his own skin began to peel away and flap in the breeze. I could hear the thuds, every one of them, hollow and deep, squishy. When his fists became useless, *Blueeyes* used elbows. It wasn't long before *Scarface* stopped struggling. His hands fell to the dirt. His eyes rolled back into his head, blood seeping from meaty wounds, cascading down the sides of his face, soaking the soil. Instead of growling he gurgled crimson, limbs limp, neck wobbly. When a bullet pelted the ground beside him, *Blueeyes* looked up from his fallen foe.

There was a man at the tree line, rifle in hand, nozzle still smoking. He was struggling to reload. He put his hand to his mouth and whistled for his companions. "Over here!"

Blueeyes rushed to my side, lifted me up, and put me on his back. "Hold on! Do you hear me? Whatever you do, do not let go!"

I wrapped my arms around his neck, legs around his waist, mashed my cheek against his bloody shoulder. The rifle fired.

We jumped.

7

It's a weird thing, weightlessness: unique. My stomach shot upward, lodged itself in my throat. I tried, tried to catch my breath and hold it. It was already gone. For a second I heard nothing, felt nothing. My hair whipped, clothes flapped. The collar of my jacket tugged against my neck. I held *Blueeyes* tighter than I'd ever held anything in my life. I locked my hands, crossed my feet, and chomped a handful of his coat with my teeth. The wind rattled my ears, worked its way inside and tickled my brain. My fingers went numb. Try as it might, the fall failed to shake me loose. The landing, however, succeeded marvelously. When we finally hit the water, it hurt. I felt it in my feet first, then my legs. The pain shot directly into my back, my arms, and my fingers. We might as well have landed on concrete. The liquid engulfed me, bitter cold. *Blueeyes* slipped from my grasp.

Everything went black.

Once again I felt nothing, heard nothing, saw nothing. Up and down no longer had meaning. Out became in. Warmth seemed silly. The moving water grabbed hold, violently tossed me. It mashed me into something solid and then into something else. When I screamed, I inhaled my surroundings. It filled my lungs, choking me from the inside out. For a moment there was a tease of air. Frozen wind stabbed my face, liquid lungs spewed. I screamed, reaching for everything, anything. The icy water reached back, took hold and refused to let go, pulled me under once again. My arm smacked something stiff, instantly went numb. Again I tasted air, and again it was taken away. It was no use. I was going to die. The *nasties* weren't going to kill me. The *nasties* wouldn't have anything to do with it. I wasn't going to be beaten, or eaten, or left in pieces somewhere along the road. I was going to drown. I was going to die in a river. I was going to die alone, just like Mother, just like Father.

Or not.

Something snagged my jacket, hoisted me from the swirling depths, and pulled me to solid ground. I couldn't see, couldn't open my eyes. Breathing was impossible. It didn't matter. I didn't need to see the face of my savior to know who it was.

"Come on! Come on!" So gravelly, that voice, so far away yet so recognizable. *Blueeyes.*

There was a sharp pain in my chest and then another, palms hammering my ribs. The vaguest sensation of lips, foreign breath in my lungs.

"God damn it! God damn it, come on!"

Everything inside rushed upward, coughed from my mouth before splashing onto my face. When I sat up, he rolled me to my side, patting me on the back. "You're okay. Cough it out. Going to be fine. Get it all out."

In between the hacking coughs, I apologized. I told him I was sorry, said I'd never do it again and begged for forgiveness. I meant every word of it. It was stupid, screaming. It nearly got us killed. I needed to stop being stupid.

He told me to *shut up.*

Though every part of me was sore, and bruised, and cold, and stiff, I forced myself to stand. My legs wanted the opposite, had other ideas, nearly went limp. I told them to *shut up. Blueeyes* helped. He made sure I was capable of remaining upright before he let me go. When I was steady, he turned his attention to the surrounding forest.

When he sighed, I could see his breath. He ran his hand through his hair, across his face, and down his beard. "We can't be down here, not this late. This is *howler* territory."

Through weary eyes, I gazed at the sky. It was dark, getting darker. Night was approaching. The familiar roar of a *howler* echoed throughout the canyon, bounced off the surrounding cliffs and back again. When I shivered, it had nothing to do with the temperature.

Blueeyes grabbed my arm. "We need to move."

To my surprise we moved further into the forest. *Blueeyes* claimed there wasn't enough time to make our way out before nightfall, and wandering around in the dark wasn't an option. We searched for at least fifteen minutes before he found what he was looking for. It was a tree, the largest and healthiest we'd come across, sturdy.

He pointed to a branch thirty feet up. "There."

I was confused. "There what?"

"That's where were staying." His hand landed

between my shoulder blades, nudged me forward.
"Climb up."

It seemed high, really high.

When I didn't move, he nudged me again.
"Anything remotely resembling human in those
things is gone. They're big and fast. They're also
terrible climbers. The higher we are, the safer we are.
Stay down here and we're food."

Before I could object, he placed his hands under
my armpits and lifted me to a branch just above his
head. I pulled myself up. I slid along the tree's limb,
legs on either side, hugged the trunk, and managed to
stand. I couldn't let *Blueeyes* down, not again, not after
the screaming incident. I wouldn't let him down
again. After taking a moment to gather myself, I
climbed. The pain in my arm was unbearable. My
fingers hurt. When I moved them, I thought I would
scream. When I grabbed hold of the branch above
me, they hurt more. When I pulled myself up to the
next branch, I wanted to cry. I wanted to collapse,
drop to my knees and sob until the pain went away.
By the time I reached my destination, I wanted to die.

Blueeyes was right behind me. He moved to a
similar branch to my right. As he settled in, the limb
bent forward, bark chipped loose, aged wood cracked.

"Will that hold you?"

"It'll be fine."

He reached above him, pulled away a few longer, straighter branches from the trunk, and set them on his lap. After retrieving the knife from his belt he began sharpening the ends into points. I looked through the twisted treetop above at the darkening clouds. The moonlight had all but disappeared. Darkness was closing in. Soon I wouldn't be able to see ten feet away. Soon the *howlers* would emerge, hungry, screaming at the sky. The pain in my forearm was getting worse. I bit my lower lip, winced and massaged it gently.

Blueeyes noticed. "Are you alright?"

"M-my arm." I didn't want to tell him.

He grabbed my hand, pulled it to him. "Let me see."

For at least a minute his fingers poked my skin.

"Does it hurt here?"

"How about here?"

"What if I do this?"

All of them hurt, everything he did, everywhere he poked. I tried my best to hide the pain, determined not to cry. I just wanted him to stop.

He let go of my arm. "Not broken…hairline fracture, maybe." He removed his jacket, put it around my waist, and tied the arms around the trunk of the tree. "In case you fall asleep…in case the *howlers* find us and try shaking you loose." It was tight, so tight I could barely breathe. I wasn't going anywhere.

When he was done, he returned to his knife and his sticks and the task at hand. The clouds roared. A stiff breeze shook me to the core. I shivered—couldn't stop shivering—and buried my face in the neck of my jacket. *Blueeyes* didn't seem to notice the cold or the fact that he was soaking wet and no longer had a jacket. He never noticed. He never complained.

"Won't you be cold?"

"I'll be fine."

The arm of his sweatshirt was soaked in blood, some dried, some fresh, black and red cascading from the bullet wound in his shoulder.

"Does it hurt?"

It looked like it hurt.

"What?"

"Your shoulder, does it hurt?"

"It's fine."

His response was always the same. No matter how he was feeling or how much pain he was in, his response was the same. The weather was of no importance, the bullet barely a bother. The *howlers* were riled up, barking back and forth, moaning at the hidden moon, empty-bellied. I stopped asking questions. At some point during the night, somehow I fell asleep.

It was the growling that woke me.

When I opened my eyes, *Blueeyes'* hand was over my mouth. His attention was on the ground below, on a shadow moving through the grass, massive, hunched, plodding on all fours. It was a *howler*. My heart sputtered, stopped. I couldn't blink. Couldn't breathe. The creature sniffed the dirt, lifted its head for a moment, scanning the forest. It was so big, so thick, yet it moved with such grace, so deliberate. It was a weapon, muscles tensed, ready to strike. The corner of its lip quivered and raised, bent teeth exposed, drool slipping from its snout. When it found nothing, the *howler* returned its nose to the ground. It could sense our presence, the faintest hint of our after-scent in the dirt. It knew we were somewhere, it just didn't know where. A paw the size of my head and claws the size of my nose kicked the dirt in frustration. I looked away, turned my eyes to the trees and the clouds, stared into the darkness and tried to pretend it was all that existed. I couldn't bring myself to see the creature below, even to acknowledge its existence. I looked everywhere else, at everything else. When I couldn't even handle that anymore, I closed my eyes.

When the growling, and sniffing, and panting began to fade away, I thought it was over. I figured we'd gotten lucky, that it somehow missed the obvious and went on its merry way. When *Blueeyes'* hand slipped from my mouth, I assumed we were safe.

Assumptions are stupid.

The *howler* slammed the full weight of its body into the trunk of our tree and nearly tossed me from my perch. If *Blueeyes* hadn't tied me to the trunk, I would have been dead. I would have been ripped in half, torn in two and left for the forest. I would have been dinner.

The tree shook again. *Blueeyes* stood. "Hold on! Whatever you do, just hold on!"

I spun around to face the trunk and wrapped my arms around it, mashed my face into the bark. The howler smacked against the base again, rose on its rear legs and scratched at the side, wrapped his mouth around it and bit down. Dead branches shook loose from above, bounced off my head. When I looked down, the *howler* looked back. Our eyes met. I swear I could see it smile.

Growls changed to barks. It lowered its head, lunged forward, and wrapped its shoulders around the trunk. *Blueeyes'* branch snapped beneath his feet just as he leapt to another. The moment he had his footing, he lifted a spear over his head, coiled back, and launched it at the monster below. The weapon sliced through the flesh of its hairy back, into the muscle underneath. It screamed. It leapt back, jaws snapping at the air, front paws flailing wildly, trying desperately to knock loose the weapon protruding from its back. While it spun and yelped, another spear pierced its leg. The *howler* snapped it loose immediately. It rammed its body into the base of the tree once more before charging into the darkness.

He had done it. *Blueeyes* had scared it off. He fought one of them off. I wanted to scream. I wanted to clap my hands. I wanted to jump up and down. For the first time in a very long time I wanted to smile. And I did.

When I turned to look at *Blueeyes,* he wasn't where he should have been. The branch he'd been perched was gone as well. The *howler's* lunge knocked it loose. He was on the ground. He was on his back. The darkness growled. A pair of deep red eyes emerged from the shadows. They were low to the ground, looking right at him.

Blueeyes noticed them too, and was on his feet immediately. "The spears, Megan! Throw me the spears!" He was pointing at a branch beside me, spears caught in twisted limbs, dangling just out of his reach. The shadow's growl transformed into a snarl. The *howler* wasn't done with us, not by a long shot. It was going to attack. I leaned to my right, reached for the bundle of spears, fingers stretched. It wasn't enough.

Blueeyes pulled the knife from his pants. "Megan! The spears!"

I reached again, extending my injured arm as far as I could, so far it hurt, so far my eyes began to water. It still wasn't' far enough. Shadows barked, huffed, claws digging into soil, muscles tensed.

"Now, Megan!"

I hugged the tree again and reached my arms around, frantically trying to undo *Blueeyes'* knot. The bark scraped my face, sliced my lip, fingers working frantically. The *howler* barked. It's jaws snapped. The echo of tooth against tooth reverberated in my ears. The moment I was free from the trunk, I jumped to my feet. I didn't care about falling, didn't even consider it. I did what I needed to do, what my *friend* needed me to do, without hesitation. My jump to the branch with the spears was awkward; I slipped, landed on my stomach, knocked the air from my lungs and nearly fell to the ground. My clumsiness also knocked the spears loose. They dropped to *Blueeyes'* feet.

The *howler* charged. *Blueeyes* charged back. From thirty feet up I watched the spectacle. It was incredible. He didn't back down, *Blueeyes*. There were no second thoughts, no thoughts at all. He wasn't reacting so much as acting. This was what he did, what he was made for. Four hundred pounds of lean muscle and teeth barreled down on him, mouth wide, teeth exposed. When the creature leapt, he leapt as well. They were monsters, the pair of them, airborne beasts, single-minded and focused. *Blueeyes* screamed. The *howler* screamed back. The tip of his spear pierced the creature's belly. The forward motion and weight of the *howler's* own body sank the weapon further in, through muscle and organs and out the other side. Even with a spear through its midsection, the monster refused to relent. It crashed into *Blueeyes*, bent him backward, the full weight of its bulk crushing his chest. He squirmed underneath, attempting to maneuver himself from striking distance as the creature snapped at his head, missed, and received a mouthful of dirt. Its paws swiped at him, coming up empty. A single arm emerged from under the *howler*, knife in hand. *Blueeyes* drove the blade into its neck, twisted, pulled, and stabbed again. When the creature rolled off him, he rolled with it, stabbing and turning, jaw clenched, eyes wide, teeth bared. He didn't stop. His arms never stopped moving.

So much blood; I'd never seen so much blood.

Every time *Blueeyes* stabbed, the mauled flesh sprayed blood, soaking his arm, drenching his face in warm crimson. Eventually the *howler's* limbs stopped twitching. It stopped fighting. With a knife in its head, its eyes went blank. Its snout fell limp. It had lost. When it was done, *Blueeyes* rolled from the corpse and dropped to his knees, chest heaving, trying desperately to catch his breath. He looked up at me, howler blood dripping from his chin as if he'd bathed in it, saturated. I was terrified. I was in awe.

He wiped the blood from his eyes and nodded.

I nodded back.

It was amazing we weren't attacked again that night with all the noise we'd made. The *howler Blueeyes* killed hadn't gone silently. It had roared, fought, and clawed. It shrieked to its last breath, squealed for its life. That alone should have attracted more of them. We should have been surrounded, outnumbered, and alone. We sat in that tree for hours, back-to-back, wide awake, spears in hand. Nothing happened.

We were *lucky*.

In the morning we climbed down, collected our things, and headed east. *Blueeyes* said it was the quickest route to the road. I believed him. Early into the trip, we came across a haphazardly constructed campsite—what remained of it, anyway. There were *bodies* everywhere: pieces. *Blueeyes* suggested it could have been the reason the *howlers* hadn't come for us. They were busy, bellies full.

We scavenged what we could; dug through backpacks, peeled bloody clothes from dismembered limbs, and picked through the pockets. I was getting good at knowing what to look for, realizing what we could use and what we couldn't. I suppose I felt bad rummaging through their remains, stealing. I felt worse having to leave the bodies the way they were, strewn about, destroyed, mismatched dinner scraps. I wanted to bury them like Father had buried Mother, like I should have been able to bury him. They were people, after all. They might have saved our lives.

Blueeyes said *no,* said we didn't have time, it would be messy, that the scent of their blood on our hands would only alert the *howlers.*

I lowered my head. "Breadcrumbs for the *nasties.*"

I barely whispered it. I didn't think he'd hear me.

"What?"

"Nothing."

When *Blueeyes* turned his back, I removed a necklace from something vaguely resembling a spine. It was small and silver, with delicate etchings carved into the top. The chain was snapped, links crinkly with frozen blood. I pushed a little tab on the side and it popped open. Inside there was a picture, a girl, a little older than I was. Her hair was long, blonde, and straight, neatly combed. It glimmered white like her eyes. I'd never seen hair so beautiful, so clean and healthy. I wondered how she got it to look like that, to stay that way. She was sitting straight, chin up, eyes wide, smiling proudly. She looked like she didn't care, like nothing mattered but that moment and that picture. She looked like she'd never been hungry, or scared, or felt alone. She'd never hurt, really hurt. She never would. I closed the heart, put it back where it belonged. It wasn't mine, never would be.

She wasn't real anyway, not anymore.

By midday we found a road. By night we found shelter. I offered to stay awake with *Blueeyes*, keep watch. He insisted it was safe, told me to get some sleep. I woke in the middle of the night. It was the whine of the *howlers* that did it, like always. I noticed *Blueeyes* across the room at the window, unmoving. He was just watching the way he always did, always would. I knew I wasn't in danger, even from the *howlers*. I went back to sleep and slept until morning.

I'd never slept so soundly.

Blueeyes woke me at daybreak. We snacked on the food we scavenged from the camp in the forest. I didn't care that it was terrible, didn't care about the taste at all. I was hungry. It was food. Nothing else mattered. When we were done, *Blueeyes* checked my arm and poked it with his thumb and forefinger, watching me wince, gauging my ability to work through the pain.

"How does it feel?"

"I'll be fine."

He didn't smile. *Blueeyes* never smiled. "Good." He didn't need to. I knew what he meant.

We made good time that day, kept a steady pace. I stayed close to *Blueeyes,* no less than a few feet away at any given time. When he moved too fast for me to keep up, I moved faster. I didn't complain, didn't question, over think, or complain about my feet hurting. I just walked. When I felt like I couldn't walk anymore, I did it anyway. I made sure to keep an eye on my surroundings, watched for unexpected movements, for anything unusual. I tried to remember where we were and where we'd been, constructing mental images in my head and repeating them until I couldn't forget. I listened closely to everything. I wanted to be better for *Blueeyes.* I had to be better. After four or five hours of walking, we stopped and took shelter in the half-crumpled remains of a building with a faded sign on the roof. I told *Blueeyes* I was fine, that I didn't need to rest, that I could keep going.

He told me to *shut up*.

The remainder of the day was uneventful. We walked and walked some more. At one point we made our way through the remains of a small town, crumbling buildings flanking the road, bloodstained concrete under our feet. Everything was charred, stained with soot and gun power, the faraway scent of ash clinging to the breeze. I found them interesting in a way, the remains. Peculiar. I never knew the world before things went *bad,* can't honestly say *I* understood it. None of it made sense. Nothing seemed to go together. Everything was labeled. Using bits of information Father and Mother let slip over the years, I tried to imagine what the buildings might have looked like before they were burned to the ground, how tall they were, what they were used for. Can't say I ever really succeeded. How could I? My only frame of reference was confusing images of golden-haired girls in lockets alongside childish flights of fancy. It was pointless, silly, all the stupid labels and comforts, all the beds. Everything *important* and easy was gone, turned to ash. In the end it didn't matter, none of it. They didn't matter, not any more. *Blueeyes* never paid any more attention to it than he needed to. If he didn't care about what he'd lost, why should I care about what I never had?

The sun went down. The *howlers* came out. Same as always.

In the morning we ate—nibbled really—and took to the road once again. Early into the trip we encountered a small pack of *gimps*. There were five of them plodding through the remains of a roofless building, scratching at the walls, jaws half-heartedly chewing the air. We could have walked right past them. They might not have noticed us at all if *Blueeyes* hadn't whistled. The moment he did, dead eyes lit up, feet shuffled in our direction.

I don't know why he did it. When I tried to ask, I stuttered. "Wh-what're you…?" It didn't make sense. Why did he want to get their attention? They were coming right at us, bent fingers grabbing at nothing.

Blueeyes retrieved his knife, placed his hand on my shoulder. "Wait here."

In the years since, I've learned that *gimps* are most dangerous in large numbers and when they catch you off guard, especially in tight spaces. *Blueeyes* already knew this. He already knew everything. The moaning corpses bearing down on us were spread apart, spaced awkwardly, attacking as individuals rather than a horde. They didn't stand a chance. *Blueeyes* dispatched them with ease. His breathing never changed. He never stuttered or second-guessed. He never broke a sweat. He moved and murdered, and when he was done he did it all again. It seemed so easy for him, second nature; he almost looked bored. It was over in less than a minute. *Blueeyes* used one of their tattered shirts to wipe the blood from his knife and hands before returning to my side. He passed by and headed to the road.

"You have to hit the brain." It was the first thing he'd said to me all morning.

"What?"

"The brain...only thing that kills them, all of them: *gimps, howlers,* even the *biters.* Anything else and they'll just keep coming."

I nodded.

He stopped and turned to me, glaring from above, making me feel small. "Understand?"

I nodded again.

"No, tell me you understand. I need to hear you say it."

"I understand." When my answer still wasn't enough, I added, "I promise."

It was his turn to nod.

We were on the outskirts of town when *Blueeyes* spotted the house. It was small, unassuming. The roof was just barely holding together, a half-collapsed wall in the rear. At first glance there was nothing particularly *special* about it, nothing that made it stand out from the homes on either side or the ones we'd passed by all day. If I hadn't noticed a glimmer of light shining through a partially boarded window along the side, we might never have stopped.

I grabbed *Blueeyes'* jacket, tugged, and pointed. "What's that?"

His hand went to his knife, body tensed. He hunched over, grabbed my wrist, pulled me behind the remains of nearby wall, and shoved me to my knees. When he peeked over the top of the stone, I peeked too. Beams of light flickered behind the boards crisscrossing the window. They flickered again, crooked shadows in dying grass. Someone was inside. Someone was moving.

"Who is it?"

Blueeyes didn't answer.

"Do they belong to *Bloodboots?*"

"Who?"

"The compound. Travis?"

He shook his head, eyes locked on the house and

the flickering light. "I don't know. No, probably not. The way it's boarded up…place has been here a while."

I heard faint noises, chatter from inside, something resembling laughter. There was a fence in the backyard, crudely cut sections of chain-link, scraps of unmatched wood. It didn't seem very sturdy. A stiff wind could have knocked it over. The ground inside the fence was nothing but mud, thick, sloppy, maybe two feet deep.

In the center of the mud were people.

There were three of them, a man and a woman and someone I couldn't quite make out. They were old, older than *Blueeyes,* older than Mother or Father. Their arms and legs were pulled behind them and bound together, filthy rags wedged in their mouths, knotted behind their heads. They looked dead. What little I could see of their faces was caked in filth, bodies encased in grime. Again I pulled on *Blueeyes'* jacket.

He brushed my hand away. "I see them."

The back door of the house swung open and slammed against the exterior wall, rusted hinges squeaking. Yellow light cascaded into the yard, bathing the hogtied pair. I swear I saw one of them twitch, but couldn't be sure. A man stepped onto the porch, lit a cigarette, inhaled deeply, and breathed smoke. He was gangly with long dark hair, knotted and pulled into a ponytail. His skin was like leather, wrinkled and stiff, caked in filth. *Blueeyes* put his hand on my head and gently pushed me down, out of view. When his hand was gone, I popped back up. The man on the porch craned his head up, closed his eyes, and inhaled the night. When he was done, he flicked his still-lit cigarette at the bodies in the mud. It bounced off the woman, ambers exploding against her forehead. Her eyes opened. Her body jerked. I could hear her sobbing.

She was alive.

Blueeyes grabbed my wrist and pulled me along the wall, away from the house.

"Where are we going?"

He didn't answer.

I dug my heels into the dirt. "Wait. Where are— where are we going?"

"It'll be night soon. Need to find shelter."

When I pulled back, he pulled harder. Using my free hand I tried to pry his fingers loose. They wouldn't budge. "Aren't we going to…? I mean, shouldn't we do something?"

"Not our problem."

After a while I stopped fighting, stopped trying to get answers from my mute friend. It was pointless. He was too strong. I didn't know what I would have done anyway, didn't even know what I expected him to do. I wasn't sure why I expected it of him to begin with. We didn't know the people in the mud. We didn't know how many people were in the house, if they had weapons, or how many weapons they might have. They were strangers, all of them. Everyone was a stranger. *Blueeyes* was right, he was always right. Right?

It wasn't long after that we were forced to seek shelter for the night. Night was coming. The clouds roared. The rain began to fall heavy and thick, lightning cracking the sky. Traveling any further would have been silly. Our safe house was cozy, small, and mostly dry. *Blueeyes* built a small fire, promised to keep it lit as long as he could. He told me to sleep, claimed it was unlikely we'd be bothered, the rain would *keep the howlers in for the night.* I tried to sleep. I couldn't. No matter what I did, I couldn't forget about the people in the mud, the people we'd left behind. The sound of the woman crying, the mud on her face, the tears in her eyes; it was too much. The warmth of the fire didn't help. The lack of *howler* cries didn't make a difference. The fact that I was dry and warm only made it worse. *Blueeyes* was across the room in a half-rotted chair, staring out the window, fingers lightly tracing the handle of his knife.

Lightning flashed behind him and he lost his detail. Everything went flat. For a moment he was black, a silhouette and nothing more, a hole against the bluish sky.

I lifted my head from the floor and sat up, putting my back against a nearby wall. I felt itchy. Every time I scratched, I itched more. It wasn't going away. "What's going to happen to them?"

It took *Blueeyes* a moment to respond. I think he sighed. "Who?" He knew exactly *who* I was talking about. I could tell he knew. He was trying to avoid the conversation.

"Those people, at the house. What about the people on the truck with *Scarface?*"

He wanted me to shut up. "Go back to sleep."

"I can't."

"Do it anyway."

I returned to the floor, laid my head against wood, listened to the rain, and tried to forget. I couldn't. So many cages, I'd seen so many people in cages. With all the awful things in the world, why were people putting other people in cages? I sat up, straightened my back, and steadied my voice. "Tell me."

Blueeyes' head sank. Thunder roared and lightning

popped. When he turned to face me, half his face was devoured in shadow, blurring into the wall. His eyes narrowed, voice like nails. "The bombs scorched everything...just burned it all away. What they didn't kill died a slow death. It all just rotted and went away. Nothing grows. Everything that does is poison. There's nothing left, kid...nothing but us." He turned to the window. The sky lit up and his features disappeared. "Nothing left but animals and food."

That was it. That was all he said. It took me a minute to figure out what he meant, and when I finally did, I wished I hadn't. I remembered the faces of the people in the mud, of the woman on the back of the truck and the way she cried, the way she held her children. I remembered Father.

By the time *Blueeyes* turned to douse the fire, I was gone.

I didn't have a plan, anything even coming close
to a plan. I'm not completely sure I understood the
meaning of the word. All I knew was that I needed do
something. It didn't matter what *Blueeyes* thought. He
was trying to keep me safe, but I didn't need him to
keep me safe, not any more. I had to try. So I ran.
The rain pelted my face, saturated my jacket, soaked
through my hood and into my hair. I retraced our
steps from earlier in the day. I remembered; I'd paid
attention. Even in the darkness, even with the rain, I
knew where I was and where I needed to go. My legs
pumped, feet splashed. At full speed it took me less
than ten minutes to reach the house. When I arrived,

I ducked behind the stone wall, knees in the mud, shoes sticky with filth. My lungs were on fire, body shivering. The light inside the house had dimmed, barely noticeable through the rain, voices muffled by wind. The people in the mud were still there, tied up, submerged in slop. Near the rear of the fence encasing them was an opening. It was small, too small for an adult but just the right size for me. I closed my eyes, desperately searching for courage. Second thoughts set in, unwanted. A part of me wished I had listened to *Blueeyes*. What was I going to do, even if I reached the people in the mud, even if I was able to set them free? Then what? The sky boomed and lit up, shaking the ground beneath my feet. Then there was Father. I thought of Father, of the compound and *Bloodboots,* of what *Blueeyes* had said. My shivering stopped, hands curling into to fists. I could do it.

I had to do it.

The instant I stood, the back door of the house swung open. I ducked out of sight. A different man than before stepped onto the porch. He was larger, much larger, thick arms and bulbous belly, wild gray-black hair. He pulled a hood over his head, huffed, and plodded into the yard. I could hear the splash of his boots, even over the wind and the rain. Pulling a key from his pocket, he unlocked a door on the far side of the fence and let himself in. With a single hand he snatched one of the people by the legs. It was the old man.

"Hurry up, you son of a bitch!" The voice came from inside the house.

The hogtied man barely seemed aware of his predicament. His eyes were far away, limbs awkwardly bent, probably broken. The woman in the mud beside him screamed into her gag, contorting her body, desperately trying to squirm loose. *Bigbelly* didn't care. As far as he was concerned, she didn't exist, as if she wasn't yelling and crying, begging for him to stop. *Bigbelly* dragged the old man through the mud like a satchel, face bruised, head wet with blood. When they reached the porch, his head banged off the stairs, opened a cut, leaving a trail of crimson behind. They entered the house. The door slammed shut. They were gone.

What I did next I did without thinking. I didn't want to think about anything anymore. Thinking was stupid.

I hopped over the wall and charged into the yard. I kept my eyes on the fence, on the crying woman inside. Nothing existed but the fence, the fence and only the fence. When I hit the mud, I stopped. It was thicker than I'd thought. Each step was worse than the last. I sank to my knees, then my thighs. It didn't want me to move, devoured my legs and held me in place. When my boot came off, swallowed by the muck, I gritted my teeth and continued forward. I didn't need it anyway. I'd worry about it later. It's what *Blueeyes* would have done. When I reached the opening in the fence, I dropped to my chest, my chin leaving trails in the muck. It took me a while to reach the woman in the center. By the time I did, I was coated in mud, so heavy, so tired. When I tried to stand, I fell backward. The old woman noticed me and her eyes went wide, lit with a mixture of confusion and excitement. I dove for the rope binding her limbs, jittery fingers working the knot. Thunder clapped and my heart stopped. I leapt backward, thinking it was the door to the house. It wasn't. I returned to the knot. No matter what I did, it wouldn't budge. The rope was partially frozen, encased in crystallized mud, slippery, difficult to hold. Out of frustration I whacked it with my fist. When that did nothing, I whacked it again. I moved to her head, attempting to loosen the gag in her mouth. The fabric was frozen to her face, solid and cracked; it was like trying to untie an icicle. It was no use. It wasn't working. No matter what I did, it wasn't working. She could sense my frustration. When I let go of the frozen gag, she shook her head, imploring me to continue, eyes red with tears. My legs hurt, my arms were sore, and I couldn't feel my fingers. Suddenly I was crying. I couldn't stop crying. I turned my head from her, unable to handle the disappointment in her eyes, unwilling to show her the shame in mine.

With my eyes closed, I leaned to her ear, "I-I-I'm sorr-sorry. I'm so sorry."

She shook, begging with incoherent muffles, pleading with every ounce of herself.

Again the thunder cracked. When I breathed, I saw my breath, watched it float from my body and evaporate, taken by the night. My body went limp. I was done. I'd failed. I was useless. My head fell to her shoulder, slid into her neck. "I-I-I'm….I ju-jus-just…sor…" She never stopped begging, twitching in the mud and shaking her head. Even covered in grime, she smelled so familiar, so female. She reminded me of Mother.

That only made it worse.

Suddenly there was a hand on my shoulder, long fingers, firm grip. It pushed me from the old woman, slid me backward across the mud. It was *Blueeyes*. His knife went to the rope binding the old woman's limbs, chipped away the ice and sliced through. The moment she was free, she slammed the undersides of her fists into his chest, which caught *Blueeyes* by surprise. When he tried to grab her, she slipped through his fingers. She was soaking wet, greased up, faster than she looked.

She lunged forward, hopped to her feet, and slid the gag over her head. "Edward!" She screeched so loud it hurt my ears. The people in the house had to have heard her. Everything heard her.

Arms waving, the old woman barreled forward, rain pelting off her face, stiff limbs stomping through mud. She didn't bother to stop for the fence. I'm not sure she even noticed it. When she hit the steel it bent under her weight, twisted and popped. The entire structure crumpled. Rough welds cracked. Jagged ends tore into her skin, caught the fabric of her shirt, nearly tearing it away. She was caught. A few years prior, I'd seen a *gimp* caught in barbwire fence on the side of the road. It moaned and squirmed and reached for Father's arm when we passed by. It accomplished nothing, only made things worse. The old woman had become that *gimp*. She didn't care and she never stopped screaming. Even face down in the mud, even when the fence had ensnarled her completely, slicing into her skin and tearing her to pieces, she never stopped screaming.

Blueeyes pushed me face-first into the filth. "Stay down! No matter what, you stay down!"

The back door opened. *Bigbelly* stepped out. He was holding a shotgun. His eyes immediately went to the old woman. "Motherfuc—"

I felt the gunshot in my ears, so incredibly loud it rattled my brain. The old woman's chest exploded. Her back erupted. Blood and bone and bits of charred meat sprayed backward, sprayed everywhere. Something chunky landed in my hair. Something slimy bounced off my back. Her body jerked backward, bent awkwardly over the fallen fence, and hung limp. Before *Bigbelly* could fire again, *Blueeyes* was on him. He lunged forward and knocked the weapon from the larger man's hand while burying his knife wrist-deep in his bloated midsection. Before Bigbelly could react, he stabbed again. *Blueeyes* held him upright while stabbing and shoving him back into the open door.

I didn't see what happened next, only heard it. There was a gunshot and then another, a flash of light. Someone screamed. Something shattered. A roar of thunder hid the rest. It was a minute before *Blueeyes* emerged, jacket soaked in blood, beard stained red. He looked at me, looked past me. Without a word he moved to the body of the old woman.

I didn't know what to say. "A-are you…?"

With one hand he snagged her by the hair, lifted her head. With the other, he drove his knife through her skull.

I froze.

"Everything comes back, Megan." He stepped over the corpse and moved to the body still hogtied in the mud. It was a man, younger than the others, alabaster skin, red sores along his arms. *Blueeyes* put his fingers to the man's neck, searching for a pulse. When he found none, he put a knife in his brain. "*Gimps, howlers, biters*…we all come back as something."

I wanted him to yell at me. I wanted him to scream and leave me there, alone in the mud, alone with the dead. He didn't. Instead he helped me up, knocked the globs of mud from my jacket, turned my face up, and let the rain wash away the filth. He should have smacked me, should have put his knife in my skull as well. I wanted him to. It would have made things easier. I told him I would never mess up again. I lied. He didn't even shake his head.

He barely looked at me.

When *Blueeyes* finally spoke, it was to the night, to empty space. "We need to take what we can from the house…need to be quick about it. Gunfire will have riled up anything nearby, rain or not."

I followed him inside without a word. The house was a mess, blood everywhere, broken glass and snapped wood. A pot of still steaming liquid had spilled onto the floor, soft steam rising from the puddle. In the corner a man's body was bent over a table, chest gushing blood, a knife wound between his eyes. A few feet away lay the corpse of the man we'd seen earlier in the day—at least, I think it was. It was contorted in such a way it was nearly impossible to tell. The upper half of his body was soaked in blood, his face a mess of meat and shattered bone. When the smell hit my nose, I retched. It was awful: decaying meat and sweat, exhaustion and hopelessness. I plugged my nose. It didn't help.

Blueeyes retrieved a satchel from a hook on the wall and tossed it to my feet, keeping a similar one for himself. "Fill it with whatever you can. Quickly."

I didn't know what to take; I didn't want to touch anything. Everything was jumbled, messy, coated in grime. I pulled my jacket over my nose, hoping to disguise the smell. That didn't work either. There were knives everywhere, every shape and size, dried blood and dulling blades. My eyes began to hurt: something in the air, acrid, disgusting. I grabbed what I could and tossed it in my sack, figured *Blueeyes* would sort it out later. Near one of the windows I found a box of bullets, near the other a handgun. It was sticky; when I dropped it in the satchel, it clung to my fingers. Everything was sticky. In the back of the room there was a doorway with a frayed piece of fabric doubling as a door, gently swaying in the breeze. I moved toward it.

"No!" *Blueeyes* shouted from across the room, stopping me in my tracks. He pointed to another door across the room. "Nothing in there we need. Grab what you can from the kitchen. Meet me back here when you're done."

There wasn't much in the kitchen: a few empty pots, edges charred with bits of blackened meat, each smelling worse than the last. A pile of tin cans in the corner offered nothing; the insides were bone dry, been empty for a while. The cabinets had even less: a few spoons, a couple forks and little more. With nothing to show for the trip, I returned to *Blueeyes*. His pack was significantly fuller than mine, stuffed with bladed edges and a few articles of clothing. A shotgun and a rifle hung from his back, straps crisscrossing his chest. A machete dangled from his belt, wrapped in leather, and bobbed when he walked.

He spotted me the moment I entered. "Food?"

I shook my head.

"Damn it."

A few minutes later we were done. Thankfully, there was nothing remaining to take; we had all we could carry. *Blueeyes* pulled the hood over his head, heading for the exit. "Come on. Need to get moving."

I was happy to leave. I regretted going there in the first place, for leaving the way I had, for failing my *friend* yet again. I didn't ever want to come back.

Blueeyes stopped suddenly in the open doorway and planted his feet. He reached behind him and put his hand on my head. "Back inside."

That's when I heard it, a growl. It was deep, guttural, and noticeable even over the pounding rain. I recognized it immediately. As *Blueeyes* shoved me back into the house, I gazed past his leg and into the yard.

Three *howlers* gazed back.

10

They were massive, mountainous bodies heaving, wet hair plastered to taut muscles, steam rising from their snouts. The largest of the three barked and bared its teeth, red eyes glowing in the moonlight. Its head lowered. Its back rose. Its upper lip quivered.

When it took a step forward, *Blueeyes* shoved me in the chest. "Get inside!"

He hit me hard, knocked the wind from my chest. The blow threw me back, sent me sliding across the floor and under a table against the far wall. The *howler* charged. *Blueeyes* retrieved the shotgun from his back, cocked, and fired. I'm not sure if he hit it. Everything happened so fast. The monster yelped and leapt out of range, enveloped by shadows. *Blueeyes* ducked inside and slammed the door behind him. Immediately, his hands went to the locks, all six, fingers working frantically. He'd secured three of them when a *howler* slammed into the exterior. The weight of the beast bent the thick wood inward, splintering the frame, nearly snapping it in two. The creature crashed into it again, barking at the lightning, biting at the doorknob. While the house was disgusting, it was also fortified. The door had been custom made, thick and sturdy; it could take a beating. The *howler* hit it again.

At least we hoped it could take a beating.

A window on the opposite side of the room exploded, *howler* paws smashing wood and glass, flinging debris. Claws snagged the frame and dug in. When the beast pulled the paw back, it took a section of the wall with it. *Blueeyes* moved to the exposed window, raised the shotgun, and fired again. The attacking *howler* yelped, barked, and scampered away. The door bucked again. Another window shattered. A wall on the opposite side of the room bent inward. They weren't giving up, smashing into anything they could, fueled by hunger and animalistic rage. *Blueeyes* moved to the partially collapsed window. He wedged his shotgun through an opening in the debris, firing blindly into the night. The door cracked and shuddered; the hinges snapped loose and fell to the floor. A single red eye stared at me through a newly formed opening between the door and wall, eyelids narrowed. When its pupil dilated, I shivered. When it snarled, I leapt to my feet and scurried to *Blueeyes'* side. The house was collapsing around us, walls twisting, rusted nails showering our feet. The snout of one of the monsters ripped through the debris of the window amidst a maelstrom of dust and splinters. Jaws snapped at the air, spittle flinging from hungry lips. *Blueeyes* raised his shotgun and pulled the trigger. Nothing happened. Out of ammunition, he cracked the beast on the snout with the butt of the weapon and opened a wound on its nose, blood spewing. The head of a howler crashed through the door. A bloody paw reached in and peeled away shattered bits of wood, creating an opening. A wall began to buckle, bits of debris trickling from above. They were going to get in. We couldn't' stop them.

Nothing was going to stop them.

Blueeyes wrapped his arm around my waist, lifting me into the air, and headed for the fabric *door* he'd told me to avoid. It was dark inside, lit sparsely by mostly burnt candles. In the center of the room was a steel table drenched in fresh blood. A crudely assembled drainage system ran along one side, leading to a blood filled bucket underneath. Sprawled on top of the table was the old man from the yard. One of his legs was gone, cut cleanly, pale bone peeking through a stump of lumpy meat. His chest was sliced open, ribs peeled back. On a counter against the wall, in a bowl soaked in blood, were his intestines. My stomach lurched. If I had the time I would have thrown up.

Blueeyes kicked open another door at the far end of the room and lunged inside as the roof collapsed. The rear of the house had taken a beating and couldn't handle anymore. An entire wall gave way. Structural beams cracked, snapped, and broke in half. The roof slid over the dismantled section and crashed into the backyard. *Blueeyes* dropped to one knee, engulfing me in his arms, sections of the ceiling threatening to bury us. I smelled smoke, the familiar glimmer of fire from the butchering room we'd left behind.

That's when I heard their feet, the grotesque tapping of *howler* claws on what remained of the roof over our heads.

Blueeyes dropped me to floor, pressed my chest to wood, and screamed over the madness. "Stay here! Do not move!"

My hands went to my ears, my eyes closed, and my head nodded.

Bent over, roof collapsing around him, he shuffled through the spreading fire and into the room with the old man's corpse. A wall of smoke engulfed him. The *howlers* screamed, jumping on the failing roof, gnawing at shingles, flames rising around them, thunder cracking the sky. The door to the butchering room collapsed the moment *Blueeyes* returned. He was holding something. A cloud of debris, black smoke, and dust rose from the ashes, swallowing us. When I inhaled, it filled my lungs, spread out. I couldn't catch my breath, couldn't breathe. It was too much. It was happening too quickly. I couldn't think straight, too many noises, colors. The smoke cleared for just a moment and I realized what *Blueeyes* had in his hands. It was a leg, the old man's leg. He dug into his satchel, felt around, retrieved a single stick of dynamite. He tied it to the severed limb with fabric ripped from his shirt. The roof moaned, moonlight peeking from an opening near the corner, *howler* eyes glaring. *Blueeyes* slid across the floor, flames crackling, clinging to his jacket and singeing his beard. He used the inferno to light the dynamite's wick, cooking flesh in the process. The roof buckled and a flaming support beam crumbled to the center of the room, further spreading the blaze. His jacket on fire, *Blueeyes* charged toward the opening in the corner and flung the flaming leg into the night.

The *howlers* took the bait. The monsters caught the scent of blood in the air, chased it like the animals they were. One of them captured the flaming appendage in flight, landed in the mud and chomped down. A second knocked the first aside, taking an end for itself.

Blueeyes laid his body on top of mine and smashed me into the floor, covering the back of my head with his chest.

I never heard an explosion. It rattled my ears. I felt it in my teeth, behind my eyes. My body vibrated, hummed, indescribable heat engulfed me. Surviving the aftershock was too much to ask of the already decimated house. The inferno had done its damage. The walls popped and snapped, began to crumble. *Blueeyes* scooped me up again, wrapped me in his arms, and lowered his shoulder, heading for a collapsing wall nearest us. Burning wood ripped, crunched and exploded, bathing us in embers. When we hit the ground, we rolled, sliding on wet mud past bits of flaming debris and chunks of cooked *howler* meat. I slipped from *Blueeyes'* arms, mud in my face, embers sparking my hair. I'm not sure how many times I spun. It was a lot. The world turned upside down, flipped left and right. Everything meshed together, a blurry mess of images. When I finally stopped, I still felt like I was moving. My head was pounding. Everything was sore, every inch of me throbbed. Blood trickled down my face, originating from an unknown source somewhere in my hair. When I tried to move my neck, I couldn't. When I tried to move my fingers, they refused. Instead of breathing I belched smoke.

For a moment I thought I saw *Blueeyes* stumbling around, hand on his head, a vaguely familiar silhouette against the madness. He disappeared. The back of my eyelids ate him, folded him into black. Everything disappeared. I couldn't stay awake, couldn't keep my head up. I wanted to. I couldn't. It all felt so heavy. Everything was made of lead, refusing to bend.

When my eyes finally opened I was barely aware. Everything was shifting, blurred, watery. For a moment I saw *Blueeyes,* machete in hand, swinging at a fiery *howler*. One of them had survived. The creature's face was engulfed in flame, barking smoke, spitting liquid venom, steam rising from its back. If it hadn't been so terrifying it *might* have been beautiful. A yellow-red blur of crackling combustion, the *howler* hit *Blueeyes* with its paw and knocked him to the mud. He dropped his weapon.

I'm not sure how I thought to reach for the satchel I'd been carrying, or how I managed to find it among the mud and debris, but I did. With shaky hands I dug inside, felt for steel, and grabbed hold. I'd never shot a gun, never even held one, didn't really know how they worked. None of that mattered. My brain had nothing to do with it. My body was reacting. Tiny hands gripped the handle, arms jutted forward. The howler was heading for *Blueeyes,* snarling, a swirling light dragging behind. I steadied my arms, inhaled, and held my breath. When I pulled the trigger, the recoil launched the weapon back, breaking my finger and bouncing off my head. I'm not sure I even hit the monster, or came close. It didn't matter. It was enough to get the *howler's* attention, enough to give *Blueeyes* an opening. The pain in my forehead spread out and my brain went loopy. My eyes began to close. I remember *Blueeyes*. I remember seeing him on the creature's back atop a mountain of crackling flames, engulfed, chopping away, blood everywhere. I knew he'd be okay. I'd done what I needed to do, what he'd have wanted me to do. Nothing could hurt him.

Nothing would ever hurt him.

The darkness felt good. It felt empty and new, a wonderful nothing. I embraced the sensation, allowed it to wash over me, to seep into my pores and melt away. I wish I could have stayed there.

It would have been so much easier to stay there.

The rest of the night was mostly a blur. I faded in and out. I remember the rain, *Blueeyes* standing above me, weightless in his arms. I saw the forest, the clouds and the moon. At some point it stopped raining. Everything turned cold. When I woke it was morning; at least, I think it was morning. Vague hints of sunlight warmed my face.

Blueeyes pressed something between my lips, "Gotta eat, kid." I think I swallowed, not sure. The only thing I tasted was smoke.

At some point he informed me my finger was broken. He wrapped it with a makeshift splint, told me not to move it. It was a while before the aftertaste of soot disappeared, but it did, mostly. My lungs cleared. The heaviness went away. I woke in the middle of the night and lifted my head from the floor. My weary eyes opened. Once they adjusted to the light, blurry became clear and the fog rolled away. At first glance, I recognized nothing. It was another old house, worn and weather damaged, an old house I hadn't seen before. Instinctively, I looked for light, to a window on the opposite side of the room. There was *Blueeyes,* a familiar silhouette against the night sky. He was exactly where he'd been since I met him, since he saved me from the compound, exactly where he'd always be. Nothing could change that. At least that's what I thought.

Children can be so stupid.

11

The following week things were different. *Blueeyes*
began to train me. He taught me about the *howlers*,
their weaknesses and strengths, everything I *needed to
know.* He said they usually traveled in small packs,
kept to the woods, hunted at night. They were big and
strong and fast, but maneuvered poorly. He told me
that my size was actually an *advantage,* that I could go
places they couldn't, that I could hide. If things ever
went badly, I needed to remember that. When we
found the corpse of a *howler* on the side of the road,
he sliced it open. It had been dead for some time,
rotting. Its insides were basically mush, covered in
maggots and insects I'd never seen. *Blueeyes* peeled
away the skin, showed me its bones, gave them

names. He focused mainly on the weak points in the chest. While only a blow to the brain was the only thing that would kill them, the *howlers* felt pain. They weren't *gimps*. If you cut them, they felt it. When they felt it, they slowed.

Injuries are opportunities. That's what he said.

When he finished with the *howlers*, he gave me a lesson on the *gimps*. Like the *howlers,* they tended to travel in packs. Packs could be dealt with. Bloated packs of fifty or more were a horde. Hordes were dangerous, too many hands and bodies, too many mouths. Hordes were to be avoided. *Blueeyes* explained that most people turned into a *gimp* when they died. He didn't know why, didn't particularly care. There were millions of them. That's all that mattered. Mostly, they kept to abandoned towns, shopping areas, wandering through vague remembrances of what they'd lost. *Blueeyes* hated the gimps.

He mentioned the *biters,* but only a little.

When he was fished with the monsters, he taught me about fire, and shelter, and food, basic survival. I learned what was safe to eat, bugs mostly, and what wasn't. Plants were off limits.

We turned them into poison. That's what he told me.

Howler meat was a no-no. It was dead flesh, infected, rotting. The *howlers* looked like animals, but they weren't. They were people once, just like us.

It'll be the last thing you ever eat. That's how he put it.

I never considered it anyway.

When we were low on scavenged food, we dug through the dirt for a meal. I'd never eaten a cockroach, didn't much like the taste. They were crunchy, insides like slime. The first time I bit into one, it exploded in my mouth, coating my tongue in warm goo, spindly legs twitching all the way down. Worms weren't much better. The spiders? Don't get me started on the spiders.

When we weren't walking, *Blueeyes* showed me how to use a weapon. He gave me a knife, taught me how to stab. *Stick and twist.* He made me repeat it: *stick and twist.*

"When you pull your knife out, you want to take as much with you as you can."

He made a sheath from *howler* skin, attached it to my belt. I practiced as often as I could, throwing my arm forward, twisting my wrist and pulling back. It was heavy, felt awkward. *Blueeyes* said I'd get used to it. He said I *had* to and didn't let me put it down. I needed to become *comfortable* with it. Using it had to be *second nature*, like an *extension of my arm*. Late one night, he presented me with a bow. It was crudely made, little more than bent wood and string. I loved it. He cut one arrow for me, dropped a pile of wood in my lap and told me to do the rest. I didn't sleep that night. I carved. When I was done carving, I carved some more. The next morning I asked him if I could use it. He told me to *wait*. A few hours after, I asked again. He said *later*. From that point on, I bugged him about it every ten minutes, fiddling with the bow as we walked, pulling the string and watching it snap, looping it across my chest, playing with ways to carry it.

"Can we shoot a few?"

"Not yet."

"How about now?"

"Later."

"Just one? Can I shoot just one?"

"Once we're out of town."

At some point he stopped responding altogether and left me talking to the breeze.

When I finally shot an arrow, it didn't go as well as I'd hoped. It was harder than I thought. My broken finger wasn't helping. *Blueeyes* had me aiming at trees. All I hit was air. When I ran through my arrows I collected them and tried again.

After three rounds of failure I'd had enough. "I can't do this...my finger."

"Stop complaining. You have four more."

I couldn't complain with *Blueeyes*. He wouldn't listen to it. With him there were no excuses, no second-guessing. They didn't serve a purpose, not anymore. They were relics of a bygone world, pointless. You either did or you didn't, passed or failed. If you failed, you died. The next day my shots were closer, the day after that closer still. The following day I actually hit a tree. Later that night I hit another.

When the sunlight disappeared, we'd talk. Actually, I did most of the talking. *Blueeyes* listened. It made me feel better; took my mind off my hunger pains and the wail of the *howlers* outside. Sometimes, I babbled about the weather, about how I was getting better with the bow. I talked about Mother and Father too, about the places we'd been, things we'd seen. I told *Blueeyes* how beautiful she was, my mother, about her eyes and her dimples. I told him how she would wipe my face clean, how she braided my hair one night and let me braid hers. I told him how she died, how Father buried her on the side of the road, the way her lips felt the last time she kissed my face. After that, I didn't want to talk about them anymore.

"Do you have a family?"

Blueeyes never answered. He never talked about anything other than surviving or killing, or surviving long enough to kill. He just stared. He watched the sky and the road, always scanning, always alert. For him, everything was practical. Every sentence had a reason to be spoken. There was no small talk, idle chatter. I didn't care. At some point it stopped mattering. He didn't need to respond. I was going to ask whether he responded or not.

"Are they gone, your family?"

His head lowered. He turned away from his window, staring at me from across the room. His mouth moved; hesitant lips parted, then closed.

He looked away. "Go to sleep."

I had him. Even at ten, I knew I had him. He wanted to say something, to talk about something other than monsters and weapons and where we'd find our next meal. If *Blueeyes* was capable of getting comfortable, he was getting comfortable. I saw it in his eyes, the wrinkles on his forehead, the way his chin touched his neck when his head dropped. I couldn't stop.

I reworded the question, changed the topic slightly, "What did you do? You know, before the bombs?"

Nothing.

Sitting up, I leaned myself against the leg of a nearby table. "Father didn't like talking about it either…sometimes, I guess. Once he told me he flew a lot, like a bird, meeting people in other places, staying in big buildings. Mother said he looked handsome in his *suit* and they kissed." My voice lowered to a whisper: "I liked seeing them kiss."

Still nothing.

"Were you ever in a *suit?* What's a *suit?*"

He chuckled; at least, I think he chuckled. I'd never seen *Blueeyes* chuckle and I wasn't sure what it looked like. The right side of his lip curled upward for a moment, immediately turned back. When he spoke, he shook his head. "No."

"Why not?"

He sighed. I think he rolled his eyes. I was wearing him down. "Never needed one, I guess…never had the money."

"What's *money?*"

I didn't know. I still don't.

"It was just something, paper and coins…just nonsense. We used it to buy things we didn't need for people who didn't need them. Made some of us feel better about ourselves...inflated egos, lack of perspective."

I didn't know what he meant. I didn't care. I liked the way he said it, liked listening to him talk, feeling like there was someone in the room with me. I didn't want him to stop.

"Tell me something else."

"Like what?"

"Anything. If you were never in a *suit,* what did you do?"

He sighed again and leaned back in his chair and scratched his beard. Outside the *howlers* moaned. "I guess I didn't do much...moved from job to job. I washed dishes for a while, little dump outside of town. Had a warehouse job, delivered packages around the holidays. For a year or so I was getting up at four in the morning to vacuum an electronics store, scrubbed the toilets...bloody tampons from the ladies room."

"What's a *tampon?*"

He chuckled again, more noticeably than the last. "Nothing you need to worry about." His attention moved to the window, the darkening sky: yellow, orange and crimson. "Alex was disappointed in me, had to have been. Can't say I blame her."

A name. He said a name. "Who's Alex?"

"My wife." And just like that I wasn't in the room anymore, at least not from his perspective. He was just talking to himself, to the sky, and to his conscience. He was talking to ghosts. His voice transformed to something soft, unfamiliar. "She smiled politely when I brought home those checks…a hundred bucks here, fifty there. She told me it didn't matter. She never said anything, but I could tell. Three of us crammed into a shitty apartment, thrift store clothes. Wasn't exactly what she'd imagined. I wasn't a provider, didn't take care of them the way I should have. Failure. I didn't even fight when she finally had enough and took off. I just let them go."

His face went soft. "I should have fought."

"Who's *them*?"

Soft turned hard. His eyes narrowed, back straightened. I'd asked one too many questions. "*Them* is no one." He was done.

Before I could say anything else, *Blueeyes* stood and headed for a doorway on the opposite side of the room. "Enough for tonight. Go to sleep."

He didn't return for twenty minutes.

Things were quiet the next day. He stopped answering my questions, mumbled responses with gravely breath. Late afternoon we happened across a pack of *gimps* outside an old shopping center. They were mindlessly roaming the parking lot, pawing at reflections in windows, rotted heads hanging loose. We watched them from a hill behind the twisted steel of a crumpled sign. It was nothing we hadn't seen before. The creatures were everywhere, a constant threat. They were practically traveling companions. Until *Blueeyes* told me to *get my bow,* I wasn't sure why we'd stopped to look.

"What?"

"Can't shoot at trees forever. Need a moving target."

I'd never shot at anything, not intentionally. When the *howler* was attacking *Blueeyes,* I didn't really do the shooting as much as the shooting did me. It just happened, independent of thought. The *gimps* below seemed so far away, tiny. I'd never shot anything so tiny. I grabbed my bow, hands slippery with sweat. My arms were shaking and wouldn't stop. If *Blueeyes* noticed, he didn't say anything. When I grabbed an arrow, it worsened. The jitters moved through my shoulder and into my chest, affecting my breathing.

They were too far away.

Way too far.

I stood, raised my bow, straightened my back, inhaled, and held my breath. For a moment, I closed my eyes. A part of me wished the *gimps* wouldn't be there when I opened them, that I could go back to shooting trees and annoying *Blueeyes* about letting me shoot trees. It didn't work. They were still there, foggy eyes staring at nothing in particular, torn flesh flapping in the breeze. They were like the dirt, like the rain or the wind. They were always going to be there. I scanned the group and settled on a particularly large one near the back. One of his legs was bent backward, dragging along the pavement, a trio of dusty bones protruding from an open chest. I named him *Oneleg,* repeated it in my head. I'm not sure why. Despite the distance I could hear him moaning in that soft-sad way all *gimps* moaned, like starved animals, lonely monsters waiting for *something.* I was putting him out of his misery. That's what I told myself.

It was mostly true.

When the wind died, I fired. The arrow bounced off the roof of a car, flipped, spun through an open window. Absolutely none of this happened in the vicinity of *Oneleg.* A few of the *gimps* heard the noise, saw the arrow sail into the building, moved in its direction.

Blueeyes handed me another arrow. "Try again."

I loaded it, aimed, inhaled, and fired. I hit a brick wall. "I'm sorry."

He handed me another. "Shut up. Try again."

Fifteen arrows later and I hadn't hit a thing. Thankfully the *gimps* hadn't caught on. I'm not entirely sure what they thought of the random arrows bouncing off everything or if they were even capable of putting it together. Probably not. As long as they didn't see us or smell us, we were safe. *Oneleg* continued to limp around without a care in the world, arrows breezing past his head, slamming off garbage cans and crashing through windows. He was mocking me and he didn't even know it. I swear, *I swear* I could see a smile on his face. *Blueeyes* stood, dropped a bundle of arrows to the dirt, unsheathed his machete, and started down the hill. I wasn't expecting that.

"Wait. Where are you going?"

He didn't bother to look at me. "Down there."

"No. Y-you can't. There are too many." There were too many. They were too close together. Even for *Blueeyes*.

"Guess you better start hitting something."

They noticed him when he was halfway down the hill. Thirty heads turned in unison, thirty eyes widened, and thirty mouths opened. All at once they snarled. My heart stopped. I couldn't breathe. I fumbled, slipped, and landed on my rear. By the time I grabbed an arrow, *Blueeyes* had engaged them. He never stopped moving forward, never paused or hesitated. After killing one he moved to the center of the group, chopping and slicing, kicking them in the chests to keep them at a manageable distance. With every second the mass of hungry monsters thickened. They surrounded him, plodding inward, rotted teeth chomping. My first arrow hit pavement, ricocheted off a wall and landed in the dirt. It was way off target. Even with them crowded together, I hit nothing. A *gimp* grabbed a handful of *Blueeyes'* jacket and pulled it taut against his neck, nearly knocking him off his feet. He removed the monster's arm from its torso and put a blade through its skull. I reached for another arrow and dropped it. When I finally got it into place, the bowstring slipped through my fingers. I wanted to cry. I wanted to scream. I could barely see *Blueeyes*. A sea of *gimps* had swarmed him, an ugly, panting mass of gangrenous limbs. If he was alive, he wouldn't be for long. I needed to do something.

I didn't drop the next arrow. My bowstring didn't slip. My hands didn't shake. Again, I squared my shoulders. Again, I inhaled and held. When I felt the wind on the back of my neck I listened, really listened, afforded myself the fraction of a second necessary. It tussled my hair, tossed it across my eyes and back again. It moved over the tips of my fingers, into my hands and along my arms, and steadied my muscles. My eyes narrowed, gaze settling on a single head among the masses, wispy dark hair moving the same as mine. When *Oneleg* moved, so did my arms, anticipating. Suddenly they didn't seem so far away. They were close, so close I could touch them. It was *Oneleg's* hair on my face, not my own.

When I exhaled, I fired.

The arrow pierced his skull, passed through cleanly, exploded from the other side. No time for celebration. I grabbed another, fired again, and hit. The next shot was the same. The one after that hit a shoulder. The following attempt corrected the mistake. I didn't stop. I didn't notice the pain in my shoulder. My broken finger didn't exist. With every shot the herd thinned. With every pull of my bowstring, another body fell. Seven headshots later I could see *Blueeyes*. He was still alive, still swinging, soaked in blood, with chunks of decomposing meat bouncing off his jacket, mucus and blood dripping from his face. When only two *gimps* remained, we each killed one. Just like that, it was over. I lowered my bow. My arms dropped to my sides, my shoulders slumped. I felt heavy, so wonderfully heavy, all over. When I allowed myself to inhale, the air smelled different. It burned my nostrils, left an aftertaste in my throat: pungent copper, liquefied steel. It was awful, wonderfully awful. For the first time in my life

I was alive.

When I finally looked up, *Blueeyes* looked back.

Five minutes later, we were on the road again. My traveling companion didn't bother to congratulate me. He never said *good job* or threw a *thanks* my way. I was fine with it. He didn't need to. Nothing was different between us. Nothing had changed. The road was still there and we still needed to walk it. While I didn't fully realize it at the time, he was giving me exactly what I needed. There wasn't room for a *good job*, not in our world. *Good jobs* were silly, even for a ten year old. They were outdated. *Good jobs* were pointless and *good jobs* would only get us killed. We were too smart for *good jobs*. We had to be.

That night I slept with my bow at my side. Even gave it a name: *Pointycrunch*. When I told *Blueeyes,* he shook his head. When he turned away, I thought I heard him chuckle, couldn't be sure. *Blueeyes* rarely chuckled. He might have burped.

The next morning I made *Pointycrunch* some arrows and tightened his string. He deserved it. While I ate, I kept him on my lap. When we hit the road, I threw him over my shoulder. When we rested, I practiced. When we walked, I practiced as well. I was aiming at things much smaller than before, further away. I was getting better. It was beginning to feel natural. *Pointycrunch* was becoming an extension of my arm. Where I pointed, he crunched. What I needed him to do, he did, always, without question. I was aiming at the doorknob of an abandoned house at the end of the block when *Blueeyes'* hand smacked me in the chest and knocked the air from my lungs.

"Wha—"

The very same hand moved to my mouth. The other reached for his machete. Suddenly, he had me by the arm, dragging me to the trees. When I couldn't keep up, he lifted me into the air. The moment we reached the tree line, he threw me to the dirt. I was spitting sand from my mouth when I heard it: a truck, a lot of trucks actually. They seemed far away, old engines popping, tired brakes grinding. I couldn't tell where the noise was coming from, but it was getting closer. When I tried to stand, *Blueeyes* shoved me down. When I attempted to wiggle from his grasp, he shoved me harder. From behind the grayed branches of a dying bush, I watched the road. A massive jeep rolled into view, camouflaged in gray and white, reinforced with bits of scavenged steel, an obscenely large gun mounted to the rear. There were two men standing beside the weapon, bobbing as the truck moved, torsos thickened with body armor, gas masks obscuring their faces. A second jeep followed the first and a pair of trucks after that. Two cars, equally armored, brought up the rear. I'd never seen so many vehicles in one place, at least not ones that worked.

When I spoke I whispered, not that they could have heard me over the noise. "Who are they?"

It took *Blueeyes* a moment to respond. His attention was on the road, on the small army passing by. "Don't know."

"Bloodboots?"

"Maybe."

I didn't like the sound of that. I'd nearly forgotten about *Bloodboots,* believed we had put enough distance between us, hoped I'd never see him again.

We watched the vehicles until they vanished into the fog. The moment we couldn't hear them anymore, *Blueeyes* stood. He dug into his beard and scratched his chin, never relaxing the grip on his machete. "We can't go that way." His eyes moved from the road to the forest behind us. "Have to find another way around."

I didn't like the sound of that either.

Blueeyes sensed my unease and strangely tried to reassure me. "It'll be fine. Still early. We have time."

I wasn't particularly crazy about him trying to calm me; it wasn't like him. Even at ten, I knew he wasn't telling me everything. Something was up.

We spent the next hour trudging through the forest. I tried my best to get information from him. He wasn't having it. When he actually responded, his answers were brief, cryptic. Sometimes he changed the subject. Other times he just told me to *shut up*. Whatever he knew he was keeping to himself.

The sunlight was waning when we found the road again. The fog had thickened, moist against my face. We were in an industrial area, massive structures for as far as I could see, cracked concrete and rusted steel, ghostly towers swallowed by the mist.

Blueeyes pointed to one of the larger buildings a bit further down, surrounded by a mostly collapsed fence, its four walls basically intact. "There…we'll stay there tonight."

I wasn't sure why he chose it; it didn't seem particularly inviting. Then again, not much did. It had to be better than a tree in the forest, than another night with the *howlers*. When *Blueeyes* began walking in its direction, I followed. We entered through a crack in the exterior where the walls had shifted. While it easily large enough for me, *Blueeyes* had to contort himself a bit. Once he was through, he helped me inside. The odor hit me immediately. It smelled terrible, old and crusty, rotted. It stank of dead. There was something artificial about the air, unlike anything I'd ever smelled, difficult to describe. Instead of investigating further, I squeezed my nose. The interior of the building was massive, packed with rows of oversized metal drums. Partially collapsed stairs were spread across the hanger and led to the upper levels, crisscrossed with the shadows of a decimated glass roof.

Blueeyes motioned to a stairwell on the opposite end of the room, barely visible in the darkness. It seemed sturdy, at least more so than the others. "Up there. The higher we are the better. Should be saf—"

The shadows hissed.

We weren't alone.

Blueeyes raised his machete and pulled me close. "Shit."

Before we could retreat, the eyes began to appear, so white they seemed to glow, so many of them. They emerged all at once, flashing lights from the shadows, formless orbs erupting from the void. Something screeched, a high-pitched wail sharp as glass echoing throughout the structure. My heart jumped, muscles stiffened. Instinctively, I reached for *Pointycrunch*.

"Your weapons are unnecessary." The voice that originated from the darkness shook me. I jumped and dropped *Pointycrunch*. There was something about the inflection, the tone unlike anything I'd ever heard. Every word was stretched, every syllable desperately clinging to the one before. I could almost hear a flickering tongue.

I moved behind *Blueeyes,* hiding myself behind his leg. The white eyes stared, blinked, more of them popping into existence. Twenty pairs transformed to thirty in seconds. Thirty became forty. One of them was moving toward us, strangely brighter than the rest and growing larger. *Blueeyes* reached for the shotgun strapped to his back and pointed the muzzle in their direction.

Even with a shotgun pointed at it, the voice from the shadows remained steady. "Despite what you may have heard, we have no interest in devouring children. We are not *animals.*"

The darkness parted and something vaguely resembling a man stepped into the light. His skin was grayish-white, flaky like chalk, bloated veins like the fissures in pavement running along his skull. He was dressed in filthy rags, hanging loosely from wiry shoulders. When he looked at me, he smiled—at least, I think it was a smile. His lips curled upward, dry skin cracked. There were rows of yellow teeth extending deep into his mouth and down his throat, at least fifteen teeth, each tooth sharper than the last. His arms were gangly things, disproportionate to the rest of his body, fingers reaching his knees. His entire body was a bony mess of awkward angles. Every time he moved new lumps appeared, new bones threatening to break the surface.

Blueeyes' finger tightened on the trigger. "Close enough."

The shadows didn't appreciate the threat. They hissed in unison.

Sensing their anger, the bony thing in front of us lifted his arm and motioned for the group to relax. His face grew serious. His gaze narrowed, focusing on *Blueeyes.* "We leave the eating of children to the *breathers,* sir. You have my assurance that none among us will harm the girl." Suddenly, his chin lifted. His nostrils flared. He was sniffing, inhaling a particular scent in the air and desperately trying to make sense of it.

When he was through, his milky eyes settled again on *Blueeyes.* "And you...you're something different...you we can't eat...you're..." Blank eyes widened. "What exactly are you?"

12

I'd never seen a *biter* before. I'd seen the aftermath of their attacks, but never one in person and never so close. Truthfully, at the time I had no idea that's what I was looking at. Everything was a monster. Everything wanted to kill me, eat me. At some point, the differences between them no longer mattered. The creature's eyes remained on *Blueeyes,* wild and wide, mouth agape. It seemed confused by his very existence.

My traveling companion didn't move, didn't blink. His shotgun remained forward, machete at the ready. "What are you talking about?"

The *biter* grinned. "I think you know exactly what I'm talking about. You're not one of us, not one of them…" His bony finger pointed in my direction, and I shivered. "Certainly not one of her."

Blueeyes nudged me backward. He didn't like what he was hearing, that much was obvious. He didn't want to hear it anymore. "We're leaving."

"Wait!" There was a sense of urgency in the *biter's* voice. "Please!" When he took a step forward, *Blueeyes* took one as well.

There was no subtlety in the maneuver. *Blueeyes* would not be trifled with. He would not back down from anything, ever.

The creature sensed this as well. It lowered its arms and relaxed its stance, changing tactics. "You will not survive out there. *Howlers* patrol this area regularly. They're as much a danger to us as they are to you. Doesn't matter that they can't eat us…happy simply killing. They know we're here and stay away when we're grouped. If you're out there, alone, they will find you." He looked at me for a moment, then back at *Blueeyes*. "Maybe that doesn't matter to you, but the girl…her scent will prove…*intoxicating.*"

I hated that word. I hated the way he said it. I wanted to leave. I didn't like how he was looking at me, or the army of glowing eyes lurking in the shadows. It felt wrong, everything. I didn't know why we weren't leaving. We needed to leave. When I grabbed hold of *Blueeyes'* pants leg and tugged, he brushed my arm away.

The *biter* took a step back, voice softening in a vain attempt to sound more human. "My name is Andrew."

I didn't know why he had a name.

I didn't like him having a name.

Blueeyes shared my feelings. "Don't care what your name is."

The features on the *biter's* face softened further, eyes dimmed. "You've encountered us before. I'm not telling you anything you don't already know, am I? You are well aware of how things work. If you weren't, you'd have fired your weapon already."

Blueeyes gave him nothing.

The next time Andrew lifted his arm the shadow eyes began to disappear, slowly folding into the black. His expression changed again, almost pleading. "This doesn't have to end badly."

Outside the *howlers* wailed. If *Blueeyes* heard them, he didn't let on. His weapon never lowered, not an inch. He was thinking. I had no idea what he was thinking, but he was thinking, planning and putting things together, weighing his options. Time stopped. Everything quieted. No one moved. The whole of the world folded to the point of a pin, tiny and dangerous. I could hear my heartbeat, uneven, pounding against my chest. Faint whispers emerged from the shadows, muffled. It felt like hours before *Blueeyes* spoke.

"Touch the girl and I kill you."

The *biter* nodded.

"Talk to the girl and I kill you."

The *biter* nodded again.

"Look at the girl and I kill every last one of you."

"Understood."

Blueeyes motioned to the shadows, to whispers from the abyss. "Make sure they know."

"I assure you there is nothi—"

"Don't care about assurances." His finger tightened against the trigger. "Make sure they know."

"Done. In exchange for your safety I require only one th—"

Blueeyes took another step forward and mashed the shotgun barrel against the *biter's* forehead. The creature's arms went to the air, body stiffened. The shadows hissed. The eyes reappeared. When *Blueeyes* spoke, he growled. "You require nothing. You stay on your side of the building, we stay on ours, and you don't die. It's as simple as that."

It was a while before the *biter* responded and, when he did, it was without words. One of his feet timidly slid backward, then the other. Keeping his hands in the air, he returned to the darkness, swallowed. The moment he was gone, the eyes disappeared.

Blueeyes moved me to the corner of the building, nudged me to the wall, and told me to *sit*. I didn't want to sit. I wanted to do anything but sit. I wanted to help him. I wanted to leave. We were making a mistake, staying there; I could feel it in my bones. I didn't care how many *howlers* were outside or what time of night it was. The monsters outside had to be better than the eyes, better than the whispers. They were still whispering. They never stopped whispering.

I let *Blueeyes* know. "We're going to stay here? We can't stay here."

"We can and we are."

The bluntness of his response annoyed me. "No! We can't! I can—"

He squeezed my shoulders, dropped to one knee, and pinned me against the wall. His voice was measured, a hushed rage. "Quiet." Outside the *howlers* screamed. "We're in the middle of nowhere. We won't survive out there."

"But what abou—"

"You need to trust me." He was close, so close I could feel his breath on my face and count the wrinkles on his forehead. When the moonlight hit his eyes, they glimmered. "Do you trust me, Megan?"

I did. He was all I had. He was my *friend.*

I nodded.

I sat.

It was a long night. I didn't try to sleep, didn't even close my eyes. As closely as I listened to the whispering, as hard as I tried to make sense of it, I couldn't. It was almost another language. Every word ran together and every syllable elongated, stretched to the point they became unrecognizable. I could feel the *biters* watching us, their eyes far enough away to keep from being seen, yet close enough to let us know they weren't going anywhere. It didn't feel right, being so close to so many of them, being surrounded. I thought about *Andrew.* His name made me uncomfortable, the fact he even had a name at all. It was wrong. He was a monster, a *biter.* They were all monsters. And yet, when he looked at me, it didn't seem like he wanted to hurt me, drink my blood and leave me on the side of the road. He was smart, aware. He wasn't what I'd imagined or what I thought he should be. That's what bothered me most. That's what made it worse. For hours I sat in my corner, *Pointycrunch* on my lap, an arrow at the ready. *Blueeyes* remained on his feet less than two feet away, shotgun in one hand, machete in the other. His eyes never slipped from the shadows, subtle movements in the darkness. He never stopped listening, never relaxed. He was tracking them the entire time. I wondered if he could understand them, if he knew what they were saying. I was too scared to ask.

As daylight approached, the shadows moved away: most of them. Thin rays of sunlight found their way through the cracks in the roof. The *biters* didn't seem to like the sun and did their best to avoid it. In the morning light, the building looked larger. The top floors were overrun with *biters*. There must have been fifty scattered through the complex, asleep on steel beams thirty feet up, huddled in densely shadowed areas. Occasionally one of them would glance in my direction, blank eyes staring, gray tongue dragging over cracked lips. Most of them were old, sickly, on the brink of starvation. They looked like they were dying again. When one of them waved, I didn't know how to react. It was a *she*, a child, not much older than me. Until that moment I had no idea there were *biter* children. Suppose I never considered it. Her hand lowered and her lips curled upward. She was smiling.

Why was she smiling?

Before I could put any more thought into it, the ceiling exploded. Stone turned to pebble, steel to shards, everything engulfed by a cloud of dust. It was loud. I felt it in my bones, in my chest and down my legs. My hands went to my ears, flaming bits of sand and debris crisscrossing the sky. When *Blueeyes* screamed, I couldn't hear him. His mouth opened and a hum emerged, steady and unending. I felt something warm against the palm of my hand. It was blood. My ears were bleeding.

The *biters* in the rafters scattered, leaping for the shadows, their home crumbling around them. A flurry of bullets riddled the wall beside me, tearing through stone, ricocheting off iron. *Blueeyes* wrapped me in his arms, devouring me with the whole of his body, gunfire popping around us. Something else exploded. Something collapsed. *Blueeyes'* body jerked. Warm blood sprayed my face, soaked my hair. Suddenly, I was airborne, everything around us bending inward, everything on fire. Twisted steel swung from a cloud of soot and missed us by inches, obliterating a nearby wall. Everything turned to dust, smoky and thick. When I inhaled, it coated my insides. When I coughed, it wouldn't let me stop. A chunk of concrete slammed into my skull. Three of them bounced off *Blueeyes*. Through the cloud of debris I saw guns, so many guns. They were outside the building,

141

silhouettes against the morning light, flashing just beyond the smoke. They were moving closer. I mashed my face into *Blueeyes'* chest, *Pointycrunch* wedged between us. His shoulder tore open, belched red. A bullet had torn through cleanly, coating his arm in crimson and bits of bone. He grunted, lurched, and grit his teeth. He never stopped moving. A chunk of his leg ripped away. A bone in his forearm snapped in two.

Riddled with steel and engulfed in flames, a pillar near the center of the building collapsed and folded in half. Most of the second floor followed. When it fell, the biters fell with it. The ringing in my ears disappeared as quickly as it had come. Suddenly, I could hear everything, the guns and the explosions, the high-pitched wailing of the *biters.* One of the creatures leapt over our heads, screaming, fingers coiled into fists. I watched as it navigated the flames, exited the fiery structure and charged the firing squad outside. Within seconds it was dead. The bullets hit it all at once, everywhere. When the *biter* hit the ground, it did so in pieces.

Something else exploded. Something fell. A bullet whizzed past the back of my head, so close it tossed my hair. There was too much happening, too much to take in. When I looked up at *Blueeyes,* his face was soaked in blood. His shoulder was unrecognizable, a chunk of pulsating meat splattered with black. We passed through a wall of smoke and found a wall of fire. In the middle were a group of *biters,* flames whipping around them. Their white skin had turned black, charred and peeling away, heat blisters popping. One of them looked at me, tears in his eyes, fingers scratching at burnt flesh. Before he crumpled to the dirt, he reached for me, through the flames and the smoke, as if there were something I could do.

He was wrong.

"This way!" Somehow the voice rose above the madness. It was *Andrew.* He was standing in an opening in the floor, eyes wide, impossibly skinny fingers waiving us in his direction. "Hurry!"

Blueeyes didn't move. I felt his body tighten, weighing his options. The gunshots were getting louder. Another section of roof broke loose, crumbling onto the *biters* already trapped beneath, shards of glass like rain. The structure wouldn't last much longer. It should have fallen minutes ago. I heard voices, faint, angry, from outside the confines of our fiery abode.

"Move in!"

"Burn those sons of bitches!"

A flurry of gunfire shattered the concrete behind us. Steel ripped, spewing steam. More *biters* screamed.

Andrew grabbed my forearm and pulled. "We have to go!"

Blueeyes didn't pull back. We rushed past the *biter,* descended into the darkness. He followed us inside, closed the trapdoor, and locked it. With the next explosion, everything shook. It was all coming down. The trapdoor above us bent inward, nearly snapped in two. Black smoke poured into our tiny hideaway. *Blueeyes* pulled my face into his chest, his hand on the back of my head, fingers wrapped in filthy hair.

"Follow me! Stay close!" *Andrew* hurried past us. Unable to see him, *Blueeyes* followed his voice and the faintest hint of his translucent eyes. The underground tunnel was cramped, no more than five feet wide in any direction. The walls were uneven, lumpy, as if they were dug by hand and dug in haste. As we moved deeper, the screams from above faded away. The gunshots slowed. Only the shuffling of *biter* feet remained. I pulled my face out of *Blueeyes'* chest and inhaled. The air was stale and stank of decay, of things dying and already dead. I didn't like it. With my legs wrapped around his waist, I clutched his jacket. His back was soaked, slippery with blood, torn fabric flapping. I traced the bullet holes with my fingers, too many to count. I didn't know how he was standing. He shouldn't have been standing. He shouldn't have been breathing. I shouldn't have been able to hear the heart pounding in his chest, feel his lungs inflate and his breath against the top of my head. He should have been dead.

Even at ten, I knew he should have been dead.

Immediately I thought of *Andrew,* the things he said and the uncomfortable way he looked at my friend.

"Are you okay?" *Blueeyes* lowered me to the ground. I felt his hand on my face, running along my cheek, over my head, down my neck and across my arms. "Are you hurt?"

He was worried. I could feel it in his fingers, hear it in his voice. He spun me around and slid his hand down my back. He was nervous. I didn't think he could be nervous.

"I'm fine."

"Good."

In that moment it didn't matter why he wasn't dead. I didn't care.

He just wasn't.

We were in that tunnel for most of the day, shuffling through the darkness, following the sounds of *biter* feet and *Andrew's* voice. I stayed behind *Blueeyes,* one hand holding his, the other gripping *Pointycrunch.* The tunnel finally opened into a room.

The area was dimly lit, enough to see a few feet in front of us and little else. The floor was tiled, littered with debris, and stained an ugly yellow that had once been white. We followed *Andrew* through a door at the opposite end and into a hallway with smaller rooms lining the sides. Whatever this place was, it was old. Everything was warped and cracking. The floor was uneven, sometimes unfinished. One moment we were walking on tile and the next, dirt. There were *biters* everywhere, grimacing as they nursed open wounds, huddled into shadowy corners. When we passed, they looked up, eyes narrowed, staring back in anger. They didn't want us there. That much was obvious. In a room near the end of the hall, shivering in the arms of a female *biter,* was the little girl who'd waved at me. She was drenched in blood, painted red, tears pouring from her eyes as she sobbed into the chest of her companion. Her arm was gone, just gone. A bloody stub remained, jagged bits of cracked bone emerging from the messy mound of flesh like a broken twig. I stopped walking. I didn't move, couldn't move. I couldn't look away. Through tear-soaked eyes she glanced in my direction, her body shaking, lips quivering.

For some reason I waved.

Blueeyes grabbed me by the arm and jerked me forward. "Megan, come on."

He moved me in front of him, hand on my

shoulder, keeping me close. "Who were they?"

Andrew's voice was steady, frustrated. "*Breathers* from the north. They've been attacking us for years, following us…won't let up." He stopped, paused, lowered his head and sighed. "I have a…*history*…with one of them."

Blueeyes' tone was similar. "Travis."

Bloodboots?

Andrew seemed surprised. "Yes…how did—"

"Prick has *history* with a lot of people. Still…seems like a long time to hold a grudge."

Andrew turned away. "Not for him."

We entered a room at the end of the hallway and *Andrew* locked the door behind us. It was cleaner than anything we'd seen to that point. It seemed out of place. Wherever we were, it didn't belong there. The countertops were white, freshly wiped, and covered with carefully placed glass tubes and needles in containers built to hold glass tubes and needles. On the wall to the left there were stacks of round containers, capped and labeled with words I didn't recognize. Everything was organized. Everything was neat. I'd never seen anything so neat.

Andrew moved to the center of the room. He leaned against a table covered in stacks of paper and motioned toward a door at the rear of the room. "You can't stay here, not after that. We are civilized, but only within reason." His eyes moved to me and settled, unblinking. "They're riled up. They're hurt and hungry. They're angry and they'll smell her. They're already smelling her. I'm already smelling her. It's too much to ask of them." His hand went to his neck and rubbed. He licked his lips. "I-I can't—I can't be held responsible."

Blueeyes squeezed my shoulder so hard it hurt, shoving me toward the door.

Andrew stepped away from the table and into our path, keeping his distance, tying his best to avoid eye contact with me. His attention moved to *Blueeyes*. "Before you go…I need to know."

Outside the room I heard the whispers.

Blueeyes heard them, too. "Need to know what?"

"I need to know what you are. I need to know *how* you are…what you are." His tone changed drastically, soft, almost pleading. His hands folded in front of him, palms mashed together, fingers pointed upward. I'd seen the gesture before. I woke up one night to Mother at my side making the very same gesture, whispering to herself. When I asked her what she was doing she placed her hand on my head and smiled softly.

Go back to sleep, princess. I loved my mother's voice, her mouth, and her dimples.

I missed her dimples.

When *Blueeyes* didn't respond, he continued. "I wasn't always this…none of us were. You know it as well as I. I was a scientist, a doctor. I had a family, a wife…" For the briefest of moments his eyes drifted to me. "…children."

He huffed and looked away. "I spent years searching for a cure. I went where they told me and did what they asked. I did everything, gave up everything. When things went bad, they went back quickly. Eventually it all went away."

When *Andrew* took a step forward, *Blueeyes* snagged me by the collar, maneuvered me behind him.

Andrew was becoming more animated, hands gesturing, eyes wide. "I was close. I was always so close. Every time we thought we'd figured it out, there was something…always something missing. We needed something to base the equations against, something new to compare them to…something we couldn't create in a lab."

He was inches from *Blueeyes'* face. "I don't know what you are, but I know what you aren't. You aren't one of us or them. You aren't like her. You're something new. You're exactly what I've been waiting for."

It was a long while before *Blueeyes* responded, fingers drumming lightly against the machete hanging from his belt. I wasn't sure what he'd do. A part of me expected him to chop *Andrew's* head clean off, grab me by my shirt, and make a break for it. "I'm not what you think I am."

"I saved your life."

"No you didn't."

"Maybe not, but I saved hers."

Blueeyes' fingers stopped drumming. "What do you want to know?"

Of all the things I expected him to do, I never expected that.

13

For the ten minutes we listened as *Blueeyes* told his story. He never sat down. He never moved or blinked. He just stood there, bleeding.

He was living alone when the *gimps* tore through the safety wall surrounding his city. It lasted longer than anyone thought it would. The world was a mess at that point, infested with monsters and getting worse. He made his way across town, staying one step ahead of the horde, through streets littered with bodies, solitary *gimps* feasting on the slow and unlucky. He found his wife at her apartment, locked in her room with their daughter at her side. He pounded on the door for an hour before she answered. Once inside he begged them to leave, tried desperately to convince his wife the city was no longer safe. They needed to get as far away as they could, quickly. She wouldn't listen. She had stopped listening years ago. When he tried again, she told him to go. When he refused, she shoved him. When he grabbed his daughter and threatened to leave without her, she smacked him.

Daniel is coming back! She kept screaming it, kept saying his name. *We're not going anywhere until Daniel gets back.* He hated that name.

Daniel was her new boyfriend, part of the reason she'd left in the first place. He was the one who'd saved her, rescued her from her loveless marriage, and gave her a reason to exist. He was the one who made her feel loved. She called *Blueeyes* a *loser,* a *bum,* told him it was *too late to pretend he cared about what happened to them.*

If anyone's leaving, it's you! That's what she'd said, eyes soaked in tears, hands balled into fists. In the other room his daughter cried.

It had nothing to do with the monsters outside.

Unable to convince her, *Blueeyes* insisted that he stay, at least until Daniel returned. She didn't want him to. He didn't care. Day turned to night, night to day, and back again. The situation outside worsened. The power failed. Daniel wasn't coming back. On the third day they heard screams from the apartment

above them, animalistic, almost a howl. They lasted
for hours. All day long fingers scraped the windows,
clawed the door. When the *gimps* weren't scratching
and clawing, they moaned. When they began
moaning, they never stopped. It was too late. There
were too many of them. They were everywhere. The
city was overrun. Escape was no longer an option.

Realizing this, *Blueeyes* boarded the windows and
fortified the door as best he could. He constructed
weapons, simple things with the little he had available.
He didn't know what he was doing. He wasn't a
fighter or a soldier. He wasn't anything. The weapons
weren't very good, poorly conceived and constructed.
He imagined escape scenarios, ways he could get both
his wife and daughter from the apartment and
through the city to safety. They were silly ideas
mostly, overly optimistic.

Days passed, then a week. They were running out
of food. His wife became more distant, irrational, and
mean. When she wasn't crying or cursing, she threw
things. She rarely slept. Sometimes he'd find her with
her ear pressed to the door, listening to the moans
and the scratching. When he confronted her, she
threatened him with a knife and managed to cut his
arm before he wrestled her to the ground. It took an
hour of screaming to calm her down.

Predictably, his daughter sided with her mother.
For years the girl heard only the worst about her

father, things he'd forgotten, mistakes he'd made. She knew what she'd been told. He was a *loser*. He was a *bum*. Most of it was true.

Most of it.

After fourteen days the food was gone, picked clean. The *gimps* remained. *Blueeyes'* daughter was sick and getting sicker. A simple cough turned into a cough and a fever. Cold sweats and shivers arrived shortly after. The girl spent her days curled in the corner, her mother at her side, her father in the opposite room. *Blueeyes* wasn't allowed near her, not anymore. It was his fault they were stuck there, after all. It was his fault they ran out of food, his fault they were going to die. At least according to his wife. She was partially right.

Partially.

Everything changed one morning. He wasn't sure why his wife did it. The day before, she had started coughing. She coughed blood. Maybe she did it because she was sick. Maybe she was tired. Maybe she'd just had enough. Whatever the reason, one night she just opened the door.

The *gimps* were there, the same as always, waiting.

He heard her screaming from the other room, heard the moans and the shuffling feet. He heard their chattering teeth. It didn't matter that he sprinted across the room. He wasn't fast enough. It didn't matter that he brought the weapons he'd made. They weren't enough. It didn't matter that he was ready to fight them all, to kill each and every one of them to save his daughter. His enemies were already dead. By the time he burst into the room, his wife and daughter were gone as well, smothered in a mountain of decaying flesh, torn to pieces. He saw his daughter's intestines spread across the floor. She was inside out.

The last time he saw her, she was inside out.

At this point *Blueeyes* stopped talking. He didn't cry, or break down, or choke on his words. He just stopped. In that moment he wasn't there. He was somewhere, but it wasn't in that room. It wasn't with *Andrew* and it wasn't with me. The expression on his face was something I'd never seen from him before, something I'd never see again. He was hurting.

Bits of his family still dangling from their teeth, the *gimps* turned their attentions to *Blueeyes*. The corpses advanced, desperate hands grabbing, machine mouths chomping mindlessly. He fought as best he could. He swung his arms, stabbed and punched and kicked. There were too many of them. They were everywhere. One of them bit his arm, locked down and removed a chunk of flesh. Another latched onto his leg, tore into muscle, teeth clanking bone. A third ripped open his side, stingy insides stretching to their limit before snapping. Suddenly, everything was bleeding from everywhere. It wouldn't stop. His arm was soaked, torso saturated, his lower half a mess of drenched clothing and mauled flesh. Everything was slippery. When he tried to shove them away, they slid through his fingers. He wedged his knife in a skull. Unable to pull it loose, he lost it forever. No matter what he did or how hard he fought, they were winning. It was useless. They were eating him alive. The monsters shoved him backward, face to drywall, tearing flesh from his body, swallowing and returning for more. Teeth tore into his neck. When they pulled away, his neck stayed with them. He wasn't human anymore. He was food, mauled meat, muscles responding on instinct alone. He was dying. He was dead.

By sheer luck, he managed to slip away from the groping hands and the hungry mouths. There was too much blood. The monsters couldn't hold onto him any better than he could them. When he hit the floor, he hit face first, lost a tooth. Somehow he crawled through their legs and into the back room. Useless feet closed the door. He had no idea how he locked it. The *gimps* scratched at the wood for hours, tried to rip it from the hinges. They beat it with their dead limbs, gnawed it with their teeth. Nothing worked. Eventually they just stopped, probably forgetting why they wanted it to begin with.

Blueeyes remained there for days, torn to shreds,

bitten in too many places to count, staring at the ceiling and listening to the moans. He couldn't move. His arms were gone, legs useless. There was nothing left, nothing worthwhile. He was unable to do anything other than bleed.

Andrew was confused. "When did you die?"

"I didn't die."

Andrew was more confused. "What do you mean you didn't die?"

"I didn't die, didn't stop breathing...no matter how much I wanted to."

Andrew turned away and headed for the other side of the room, bony fingers scratching scalp. "You should have died. Even if you didn't...*the infection alone...* Why didn't you die?" He was talking to himself, words meshing together and transforming into *biter-speak*. It was clear he didn't know what to make of *Blueeyes'* story. Neither of us did.

When he stopped whispering, he returned to *Blueeyes'* side and gently placed his palm against my friend's chest. He felt something he never expected. "You have a heartbeat. You shouldn't have a heartbeat." His eyes narrowed. "How do you have a heartbeat?"

The whispers outside the room were getting

louder. The *biters* were worked up, annoyed with our presence, frustrated with our scent. I had no idea what they were saying, but that didn't matter. It sounded bad.

Andrew pointed to *Blueeyes'* neck. "You said they bit your neck, tore it away?"

"It healed."

"How? That's not…"

"It just healed. Everything heals."

Andrew's fingers came together in a fist, twiddling anxiously below his chin. "Pain, do you feel it?"

"I feel everything…all the time."

There was a high-pitched scream, a wail. Something pounded against the door, nails dragging along steel. The hair on the back of my neck stood at attention. We'd overstayed our welcome.

Blueeyes heard it as well, looked at me, and nodded. He was done talking and he grabbed my arm. "We're leaving."

Andrew didn't seem to care. He was whispering to himself again, shaking his head, bony fingers rubbing temples. A sound I'd never heard before emerged from his mouth, half a hiss and half a yell. One of his fists slammed against the table in the center of the room. Suddenly, his breaths were labored. His head jerked upward, sniffing the air. Whatever amount of control he'd maintained was slipping away.

For a moment his *biter-speak* transformed into something recognizable, angry and low. He hit the desk again. "You have to go."

Blueeyes dragged me to the exit on the opposite end of the room. When the door wouldn't open, he kicked it. The room on the other side was small, less than ten feet across, a circular tunnel of stone leading nowhere but up. It looked old, patches of green moss growing from cracks, strange stains a hundred years old. I craned my neck back. Straight up there was light, far away, faint beams through grated steel.

Blueeyes pointed to a ladder on the wall across from us. "There." It looked older than the walls, rusted and bent, barely holding to stone. "Go. Climb. I'm right behind you."

The whispers had morphed into something new, something animalistic, more substantial. Another *biter* wailed. Two more joined in, a chorus of awful. I immediately forgot about *Andrew,* about the ancient ladder and the very real possibility of falling to my death. I just climbed. I climbed and didn't stop climbing. I'd barely moved ten feet when the ancient thing began to creak. Something bent. Something cracked. Bits of stone crumbled from above, bounced off my back. I froze. All I could hear were wails, pounding and the cracking. There was a crash. The *biters* had broken through.

Blueeyes wedged his shoulder into my backside and shoved. "Move!"

Within seconds the wailing was upon us, below us and in the same room, echoing against the walls of the tiny chamber.

"Damn it, Megan! Move!"

I held my breath. I climbed quicker than I'd ever climbed in my life. My hands were soaked with sweat, every grab a slip, every slip a last second recovery. The ladder shook and wobbled, steel and stone stretched to the limit as the *biters* grabbed hold. I ignored it, ignored them, and kept climbing. I couldn't look down; I knew what I'd see if I did. The *biters* were getting closer. I could feel them below us, hear their fingers scraping stone. They were climbing the walls. They wanted us so badly they were climbing the walls.

Blueeyes grunted, kicking at the beasts nipping his heels, knocking them away as they lunged from surrounding stone. I heard his machete, heard it swinging and heard it connect: wet thuds, definitive endings. By the time I reached the top of the ladder I was out of breath, arms impossibly sore, legs weak. I wedged my back against the steel grating and shoved. It wouldn't budge. I shoved again, muscles straining, neck soaked in sweat. It was no use. Frustrated, I made the mistake of looking down. Below us was a sea of white, open mouths and grabbing hands. There were so many of them crammed into the tunnel and fighting for position. They weren't a *horde* so much as a *swarm*, unorganized and violent, frenzied. As I stared, a hundred white eyes stared back. Fifty mouths screamed. The *biters* weren't what I expected. They weren't *Andrew,* or his lab, or his test tubes and papers. They were more than that.

They were worse than I could have ever imagined.

A *biter* below *Blueeyes* swung at his leg; bent nails tore fabric and nearly pulled him from the ladder. My friend's boot connected with its head right between its eyes. It gushed blood. The creature fell twenty feet, limbs waiving, engulfed by the insanity below. *Blueeyes* was under me, moving upward, machete hacking and feet kicking. Suddenly, we were sharing the same space. When his palm slammed against the grating above us, it moved. Dust spewed from the edges, gravel and sand like smoke.

He hit again. "Push!"

I rammed my shoulder against the steel so hard it

hurt, felt the pain down my side and into my legs. I wanted to cry. I wanted to cry so badly.

"Push, Megan!"

Instead of crying I did it again.

It moved. A corner of the grating pulled away, lifted and snapped. A chunk of stone tore from the wall, clanked off the ladder and tumbled to the swarm. *Blueeyes* punched the grate so hard I heard the bones in his hand break. The next time we pushed it flew open. Daylight filled the tunnel. Instead of wailing, the swarm of *biters* screamed, covered their eyes, and dove for cover. As quickly as it advanced, the mass of snarling monsters retreated, scurrying for shadows. I snagged a handful of dirt, dug in with my fingers, and pulled myself onto land. *Blueeyes* was right behind me. When we were both out, he lifted the steel grating and dropped it back into place.

Blueeyes sighed, shook his head, and glanced at the sky. He shook his broken hand and grimaced. In the distance there were clouds, heavy and moving fast, black bottoms flashing. "Won't have the light much longer. Have to go."

A part of me wondered what would happen to *Andrew*. Another part didn't care. We didn't stick around to find out. I was okay with that.

The rest of the day was quiet. We walked the

same as we'd walked so many times before. We didn't talk about Andrew, didn't talk about anything. *Blueeyes* ignored me. I kept close and kept my mouth shut. I wanted to say something. I really did. I had questions, so many questions, nothing but questions. I wanted to know if he was telling the truth. I wanted to know if he was alive, if he was dead. I wanted to know about his family, his daughter. I wanted to know what he was. His shoulder had already stopped bleeding, the limp in his leg disappeared. There were times when my mouth opened, when something vaguely resembling a sound emerged. As a cover, I coughed. At one point I was coughing every thirty seconds.

Blueeyes stopped, turned, and looked down at me. "Are you getting sick?"

"No."

"Good."

He knew. I could see it in his eyes.

I think he knew.

When night approached, we took shelter in the lower level of an apartment complex on the outskirts of the first town we'd come across. It wasn't much: dark and damp, tucked away. There were no whispers, not a single pair of white eyes. Outside, nothing howled. It was perfect. As I nibbled at a bit of food we'd scavenged earlier in the day, I watched my friend with different eyes than I had before. He was still *Blueeyes,* still the man who'd rescued me, introduced me to *Pointycrunch,* and taught me to shoot. He was still my friend. At least, that's what I told myself. At the same time, he was different. I didn't want him to be different, but he was. For better or worse. There was no denying it.

Andrew popped into my head. "Why did they change like that?"

"Who?"

"*Andrew*…the *biters.*"

Blueeyes grunted the way he always grunted when he didn't want to talk. "A monster with good intentions is still a monster."

"Yeah, bu—"

"Can't change what we are, Megan."

I didn't like that answer or the questions it created. It took me a while to speak up again, and I spent the next few minutes awkwardly coughing before I worked up the nerve. "What are you?"

He didn't like the question. "I don't know."

"Are you a monster?"

"I don't know."

I didn't like the answer, so I changed the subject. "What was she like?"

I think he liked that question even less. "Who?"

"Your daughter."

Blueeyes groaned and shook his head, eyes moving to the floor. When he finally looked up, he'd stopped breathing, blinking. For a moment he didn't move. In that instant I felt like he was judging me, rethinking the choices he'd made, his reasons for saving me.

He looked away again. "She was the only decent thing I ever did."

"Do you miss her?"

"Every day."

I thought of Mother, of Father, of dimples and strong hands. "Will you tell me about her?"

Blueeyes didn't want to answer. He wanted me to shut up. I'm still not sure why he did. He was uncomfortable, squirming in his seat, scratching a phantom itch somewhere deep in his beard. "She was quiet…maybe a little shy. So smart, though. *God damn* was she smart. I'm still not sure where she got that from. Wasn't from me."

There it was again, that expression on his face. I had noticed it in the bunker with *Andrew*. For the briefest moment he wasn't *Blueeyes*. He was someone else, somewhere else, reconnecting with ghosts. Outside, thunder cracked. The clouds began to weep.

For some reason, I already knew the answer to my next question. I had known it in the bunker. There was a reason he'd saved me. There was a reason he'd gone through everything to keep me safe, and a reason he always would.

"What was her name?"

Blueeyes looked right at me, into me, and through me. When he spoke, his voice was stern, every word emphasized, every pause extended. "No more, Megans."

I was right.

14

Sleep came easily. I'd never slept so well. No matter what happened, I knew *Blueeyes* was there. If I was hurt, he would heal me. If I was lost, he would find me. If I was in trouble, he would rescue me. I didn't care what he had said in the bunker, what he told *Andrew*. It didn't matter. If he was a monster, he was my monster.

I slept so well I didn't dream.

In the morning we packed our gear and took to the road. While the cloud cover remained, the rain slowed to a drizzle. I didn't hate the rain. I hated storms, but never the rain. Everything smelled cleaner in the rain, fresher. It felt good on my face, a light tickle, a soft caress. I hoped it would never stop drizzling.

For the most part, the day was uneventful. We walked, and we walked some more. The road was empty, quiet. When we stopped, I listened to the rain on the cement, pattering sheets of steel in a nearby garbage heap. I thought of Father and remembered the way he sometimes watched the rain, the quiet content on his face. We never talked about it. He never told me he loved it. I liked to imagine *she* did.

It was midday when we passed the remains of a *howler* attack. There were four bodies, too mauled to identify. There might have been five. One of them was a woman, I think. There was a dress, anyway. The flower pattern reminded me of something I'd seen Mother wear. I didn't like that. The rain had spread the blood across the street, rivers and lakes of watery crimson extending thirty feet in every direction. There was so much of it: watered down life, washing away. I I'd seen so much blood in my life, so many variations. I was becoming accustomed to it.

"Megan, come on." *Blueeyes* hadn't stopped to look. He was further down the road, annoyed that I wasn't keeping pace.

Instead of going around the blood, I walked through.

I kept my mouth shut that night. We were in *gimp* territory and had spent the latter part of the day moving from hiding place to hiding place, doing our best to remain unnoticed. Our shelter wasn't much of a shelter at all. The house was empty and the walls upright, but the place was falling apart, warped wood and rusted nails, half a door that wouldn't close until kicked. It was the best we could find, certainly better than black streets filled with the walking dead. The *gimps* were everywhere, always moaning, shuffling feet. They weren't quiet, constantly knocking over and running into things. *Blueeyes* said I should *try to sleep*. I told him I'd rather stay awake. Sleeping would have been impossible, not with the sounds coming from outside. It went on all night, dusty bones grinding, rotted teeth snapping against rotted teeth. It never stopped. I was becoming accustomed to that, too. The moment the sun rose we were gone.

A few hours into the day, I spotted someone ahead of us, maybe a mile away, too far to discern any real detail. I pointed. "Look."

Blueeyes nodded, gaze already focused on the distant figure. " I see it."

"Do we need to turn around?"

He didn't respond, didn't look away, assessing the situation. "No. Keep your head down, keep walking."

The person ahead of us was moving significantly slower than us. In no time at all, we closed the distance. It was a man, short, baggy pants with a camouflage print, covered in filth. This shirt was short-sleeved, very thin; he must have been freezing. He seemed to be pushing a cart, metal bars and wobbly wheels, rusted welds barely holding together. Every time it hit a crack in the pavement, the cart wobbled to the right. He struggled to get it straight again.

We were a hundred feet away when *Blueeyes* stepped in front of me and retrieved his machete, holding it at his side. "Stay behind me."

We moved to the opposite side of the road and *Blueeyes* nudged me to the dirt. As we neared the man, I could hear him mumbling to himself, incoherent nonsense into the mass of gray facial hair devouring his face. He was old, wrinkled skin like abused leather, discolored and bruised. Whatever he was pushing in his cart was covered with a tarp, tied with rope, and knotted at the top. When we passed, he didn't look up. If he saw us at all he didn't let on. I noticed his hands, red, covered in blisters extending halfway up his arms. They wouldn't stop shaking.

His voice was as unsteady as his arms. "Assholes…all of them ruinedeverything…sonsofbitches…cocksucking bitches….stealmyshit…never stealmyshit again."

At the time I didn't know what any of it meant. I'm not sure he knew, either.

I tugged *Blueeyes* jacket lightly. "What's wrong with him?"

He swatted my hand. "Quiet."

The old man never acknowledged our presence, continuing instead to babble into this chin, cursing his cart, his shoes, and at one point, the sun. I listened to him for another ten minutes, peeking over my shoulder, stealing glances. Eventually, he disappeared, sinking below the horizon, swallowed by the road.

I tugged *Blueeyes'* jacket, stiffer this time. "What was wrong with him?"

"Nothing."

"What about his hands, those sores?"

Blueeyes returned his machete to its sheath and sighed. "He's sick. We're all sick."

It wasn't the answer I wanted. It was the only one he gave.

We walked until the remains of the sun began to dim. The temperature dropped, so cold I could see my breath, ice crystals in the puddles along the road. Night had arrived when we reached a more congested part of town: slightly taller buildings, abandoned cars littering the road. Everything was boarded, reinforced. Barbwire stretched along the tops of fences, wrapped over doors and looped around windows. There were words painted on anything flat, bright red and massive, none of which I recognized. *Blueeyes* noticed them, too. His body language changed.

I pointed to one in particular, four words splattered in paint, so large they nearly covered the front of a building. "What's that say?"

Blueeyes retrieved his shotgun. "It says we shouldn't be here."

Another answer I didn't want.

He grabbed my arm and pulled me to his hip. "Stay close. We need to move quickly."

Suddenly, we were jogging, darting back and forth, *Blueeyes* watching the windows on either side. We moved from car to car and lowered, dropped our backs to rusted steel, taking a moment to scanning the surrounding area before moving to the next. When I stood too straight, *Blueeyes* pushed me down. When I moved too slow, he shoved me forward. Feeling like a burden, I reached for *Pointycrunch*.

Blueeyes shoved my hand away. "No. You'll move quicker without it."

The farther we progressed, the more *fortified* the buildings became. Huge sheets of steel covered doors, bars covered windows. There was a trench surrounding one house, fifteen feet wide and filled with sludge, jagged metal breaking the surface. Suddenly, the road stopped, blocked with debris, a wall of scavenged wire and steel, warnings scrawled in red. I didn't need to know what any of it said to understand what it meant.

When *Blueeyes* moved, I grabbed the leg of his pants and held tight. "We should go back."

"Can't go back, *gimp* territory. Too many of them. Can't be out here at night. "

Just once I needed him to tell me something I wanted to hear.

Blueeyes took my hand and held tight. "Stay low and keep quiet."

We crawled through a hole in the wall between a sheet of metal and an old car door. Behind the wall everything looked burnt, charred and gray, colorless. It smelled awful. There were pillars on either side of the road, one every fifteen feet, taut barbwire linking them. In the distance the sky seemed to change from gray to yellow, a hint of red. Something was glowing. I peeked over the hood of a car, staring through the black and hearing only my breath. I saw smoke and black, tiny embers popping in and out of existence, pillowed shades of black. It was fire. It was massive. My heart stopped, then suddenly sped. I didn't bother to ask *Blueeyes* what we were looking at, didn't have the nerve to whisper. The next time we moved, we moved slower, almost crawling. Voices emerged, distant but noticeable, distinctly human. We were barely fifty feet from the glow, crouched behind the remains of a bus, so close we could feel the heat from the fire and hear the crackle of the flames.

"That should be good enough to keep the *gimps* from making a move. Let's get the kids in the for the night." A man's voice. "Parker and T have watch. Willie and I will douse this thing. You know the drill people, let's get to it!"

Blueeyes nudged me to my hands and knees, whispering. "Underneath."

I crawled along the pavement and under the bus, watching as feet moved away from the fire. *Blueeyes* slid beside me, shotgun at the ready. There were at least thirty pairs of legs, men and women and a little girl in a red dress. I'd never seen a dress before, not in real life. I liked it.

"There's a little gir—"

Blueeyes' hand went to my mouth.

At the center of the fire were bodies lumped into a pile four feet high and charred to crisp, stark white teeth visible in the black. Soon after the group dispersed, there was an incredibly loud noise, like an engine, a generator. A pair of legs joined the remaining two, dragging a hose behind it. A spray of water smothered the fire, continued doing so for at least a minute. When the engine died, the water stopped. Black runoff carrying bits of burnt flesh moved across the road and under the bus, splashing against my arms. It smelled sticky, sour, a pungent muck.

Blueeyes removed his hand from my mouth and leaned close. "Whatever happens, you stay here. Do not move until I tell you to move."

He was going to do something. I didn't know what, but he was going to do something. "What're yo—"

His hand returned. "Stop asking questions. Stay here and shut up. Got it?"

I nodded.

The next thing I knew, he was crawling past me, knees splashing, crinkled black flesh clinging to his pants, heading for the feet and the smoky remains of the fire. The moment he was in the open, he stood. Feet spun and jumped, weapons clicked, men screamed.

"Motherfucker! God damn motherfucker!"

"Put your hands in the air!"

"Drop the weapon and get 'em, asshole!"

Blueeyes' voice was steady. "I don't want any trouble." He lowered his shotgun to the watery concrete.

More feet arrived from every direction, boots splashing. More guns clicked and shifted, anxious screams. In a matter of seconds my friend was surrounded.

"Where'd you come from?"

"How did you get in here, dipshit?"

"Answer him, motherfucker!"

They were screaming all at once, caught off guard, frenzied. *Blueeyes* remained calm. "Hole in your gate. Saw the fire."

A single voice emerged from the chatter, more assured than the rest. Whoever he was, he was the leader. "So you just walk right in? That how you think shit works? Looks like you've been around long enough, buddy…you know better than that."

Even more feet arrived, more guns clicked. When I looked behind me, I saw even more on other side of the bus, pairs at both ends. There were too many to handle, even for *Blueeyes*. I tried to steady my breathing, wrangle my emotions. To keep from screaming I mashed my palm against my mouth, left it there.

"Just want passage. Nothing more." *Blueeyes* again, voice unchanging.

"I'll give you passage motherfuck—"

"Calm the fuck down, Willie!"

"Fuck you, Sam! This asshole comes trotting in here like he owns the place! I ain't putting up with that shit!"

"You'll put up with whatever the fuck I tell you to put up with! Now stand the fuck down!"

While they argued, *Blueeyes* remained quiet. His legs never moved, never retreated or waivered, never once backed down. Looking back on it now, I realize he was assessing the situation the entire time. He knew what he was doing, probably knew how many there were, where they were hiding. He was reading them, studying, watching how they reacted, and planning his next move. They probably thought they had the advantage, figured they could fill him full of holes and toss him in the fire with the rest of the corpses. If they'd known what he really was, they might have understood how wrong they were.

Tensions settled a bit and the leader of the group spoke up. "You alone, guy?"

Blueeyes took a moment to answer. "No."

Chaos again. Legs scattered, weapons shifted. A pair of boots charged my friend, feet away, probably pressing a gun to his head. "Where are they, asshole? Where the hell are they?"

"Willie, stand the fuck down!"

"Fuck you! I'm done with this stone-faced fuck!"

"I won't tell you again, Willie!"

Blueeyes' finger moved, just his finger motioning behind him, pointing in my direction. Angry heads dropped into view and guns pointed in my direction. The moment they saw me, their expressions changed.

A dark-skinned man near the front of the bus lowered his weapon, both confused and let down. "It's a kid. It's just a little kid." If I'd been anyone else I would have been dead.

The mood around the fire changed drastically

after that. When *Blueeyes* told me to, I crawled from under the bus and stood beside him. He immediately grabbed my hand and held tight.

The leader of the group noticed, lowered his weapon, and ran his hand along the sweaty brown skin of his head. "If it hadn't been for your daughter there, you're brains would be splattered along the side of that bus...you know that, right?"

Blueeyes didn't correct him, just nodded.

He stepped toward us and guns began to lower. "Name's Sam. That's Willie, Mark, T, Alan, Parker, Denise, Jersey, Erick, and a bunch of other people that'll put you down if you decide to get froggy."

Blueeyes nodded again. "I'm Bob. This is Sue."

I almost corrected him.

Sam chuckled softly, his gaze moving from *Blueeyes* to me and back again. "Bob and Sue, huh?" He didn't believe the names, but didn't care enough to bring it up. "Okay, Bob and Sue it is."

I looked past him to the smoking pile of corpses, wet and shimmering. Up close the details became clear: twisted limbs and screaming mouths, empty sockets that once held eyes, everything peeled and red, cooked.

Sam noticed me staring. "Don't worry, little girl;

they were dead long before we torched 'em. Believe it or not, the smell of burning *gimp* flesh keeps the live ones away. Don't know why it works...don't care. It keeps 'em away and that shit's good enough for me. Been two months since we had an attack." He laughed. "We're living like the old days around here."

Blueeyes looked concerned. "What about *howlers?*"

"None of them out this way...not this deep into town. *Hairy bastards* don't like being closed in."

The man I assumed was Willie moved closer; he was tall and skinny, pale skin covered in fading tattoos. He seemed annoyed, anxious, and never let go of his gun or lowered his guard. I watched his finger lightly tracing the trigger of his weapon. His eyes narrowed and locked on my friend. "You've got the *passage* you wanted, big man. Hit the bricks."

A woman moved through the crowd toward the center, short hair and deep brown eyes. Walking beside her and holding her hand was the girl in the red dress. She was younger than me, not sure by how much. Her hair was dark and curly, sculpted into two puffy balls resting atop her head. I'd never seen someone so made up, so put together. She looked like she didn't belong. She was out of place, the mountain of corpses still smoldering behind her. When I looked at her she looked away, dropped her head and stared at her feet. The pair moved to either side of Sam. The little girl wrapped her arms around his leg and buried her face into his side.

The woman coiled her arm around Sam's waist and looked up at him, concerned. "Sam?"

He nodded. "I know, baby."

I thought of Father, of Mother.

I looked away as well.

Sam sighed. "Look, I can't send you and the girl out there at night. This block is clean and the smell will keep the *gimps* away, but I can't say the same for the rest of town. As far as I know this city is overrun. That being said, I can't have you sleeping in my living room either; no offense."

Blueeyes motioned behind him. "We'll take the bus."

Willie stepped between us and turned to Sam, a finger in his face. "Like hell they will. Straight up, are you serious with this shit, Sam? We're just going to let them pitch a tent on our front lawn? Am I the only one who sees a fucking problem with this?"

Sam moved close to him, his wife and daughter remaining behind. "It's a kid, Will. You expect me to send a kid out there? I ain't doing that. Come on. Think of Alexis, man."

"Don't say that name."

Sam shrugged, shook his head, and put his hand on Willie's shoulder. "I'm sorry, bro. I'm not feeding another kid to those fuckers."

"Fuck you." Willie smacked his hand away, stomped off, and disappeared into a house further down the block.

Thirty minutes later I was on my back, staring at the ceiling of the bus and counting cracks in what remained of the paint. The seat underneath me was dusty but soft, softer than anything I'd slept on in years. *Blueeyes* was pacing, moving slowly from the front of the bus to the back, scanning the area outside. He seemed on edge. Then again, he always seemed on edge. I couldn't figure out why. I believed Sam's story of the burning bodies, believed the way he told it. It made sense. Maybe it was his wife or his little girl. Maybe it was her dress. Maybe it was because he hadn't tried to kill me, or eat me, or worse. I liked this place; I even liked the bus. It was old and rusted and creaked and shifted when the wind blew, but it felt safe. I didn't want to leave.

For some reason I felt the need to tell *Blueeyes* and foolishly believed he might agree. When he passed by, heading for the rear of the bus, I sat up. "I like it here."

"Well, don't get used to it."

"Why not?"

He moved closer to me, still watching the windows, muscles tensed, mumbling. "People are fooling themselves. Three months of quiet and they think they're safe. Playing with fire…literally."

My heart dropped more than it should have. For once I wanted him to see what I saw. I wanted to be right about something. "But the fire keeps the *gimps* away…they said it did, right?"

He shook his head. "Maybe…I don't know. *Howlers* will smell it a mile away, though."

I remembered the little girl and her dress, little white frills along the bottom. "B-but I-I thought…I-I thought they don't come to the city."

"Go anywhere if they're hungry enough. If it's not the *howlers* it'll be something else. We had no problem sneaking in here. Someone like Travis finds this place?"

I was done. He wasn't going to give me what I wanted, no matter how badly I needed it. I turned away and buried my head in the seat cushion. I didn't want to listen.

Blueeyes moved to a window, struggling to see through a pane of filthy glass while talking to himself.

"The girl…the way they've got her dressed." I wasn't looking at him, but I could feel him shaking his head, could hear it in his voice. "All that fabric…*silly*…something else for them to grab onto."

He paused. "That reminds me…we're cutting your hair. Should have done it already."

I didn't want to cut my hair.

Blueeyes stopped mumbling and I stopped listening. We'd said what we needed to say. In my heart I knew he was right, even if I hated admitting it. *Blueeyes* was always right. At the same time I wanted just one night. I wanted to pretend. I wanted to sleep on my comfortable cushion in my big metal bed. I wanted to listen to the wind, feel the remaining warmth from the fire, and feel *safe*. I didn't want to think about tomorrow, about finding food, or the road, or learning to shoot, or following *Blueeyes* wherever he was leading me. I was sick of trying to be *strong*, wasn't very good at it anyway. I wanted to think about mothers and fathers and families, and dimples. I wanted to dream about a pretty red dress. Which is exactly what I did.

Until the *howlers* arrived.

15

When I woke, *Blueeyes'* hand was covering my mouth. He was on one knee, body wedged into the space between the seats. His finger went to his lips. "Shhhh…"

I could hear them outside, huffing, sniffing, nails clanking pavement. A paw slid across one side of the bus, claws dragging over steel. The sound sent shivers up my back. Something slammed into the rear of the vehicle. The sound echoed through the interior. I tucked my legs beneath me and rolled toward *Blueeyes*. There was a snout inside, poking through the broken glass on the rear door, drooling lips and crackling tongue. When something slammed into the side, the bus wobbled on flattened wheels. It inhaled, searching for our scent, and held its breath for a moment before moving away. One of them howled so loud it hurt my ears, so long I thought it wouldn't end. Another joined in. Another. Another after that. I counted fifteen distinct voices screaming at the moon, anxious to feed, the scent of flesh in the air. There were probably more. One was too many. Suddenly, I couldn't breathe, couldn't catch my breath, hyperventilating. Everything was spinning. The features on *Blueeyes'* face blurred, twisting into something unrecognizable.

Fifteen *howlers*.

The bus jerked, old metal screeching, rusted welds cracking. A window on the front door shattered. One of the *howlers* leapt to the hood and stepped to the roof. It was above us, pacing, steel folding under its feet. I could see the outline of its paw as it moved, bent inward and molded around the massive appendage. My lip quivered and my hand began to shake. I wanted to scream. I needed to scream so badly.

Blueeyes grabbed my head, hands on either side, whispering. "Look at me."

All I heard were footsteps, low moans, and deep

growls.

"Breathe, Megan. You need to breathe."

The monster on the roof screamed at the sky.

"Breathe. You can do it."

Its body tensed, claws digging into steel, piercing and pulling back.

"Look at me, Megan. Look at me."

I looked.

"We're getting out of here. I promise."

There was something about his eyes, the way he was staring at me, the expression on his face. He wouldn't let me die, couldn't, not again. When he looked at me, he was looking at her, at everything he'd lost. He would do anything for us, for a chance at redemption. He would die to keep us alive. I believed every word he said.

My breath returned.

"That's it. Good job."

Glass shattered. A gun fired. In a matter of seconds there was anarchy. Bullets pelted the street and the bus, tearing the surrounding area to pieces. *Blueeyes* pulled me to the floor, crawled on top of me, glass shattering around us, metal riddled with ammunition. The *howlers* wailed and scattered, attacking the houses on either side, charging the flashing muzzles, absorbing steel from above. An explosion shook the ground. Another, much closer; the bus trembled. On the roof of the bus I could see the reflection of fire, crackling shadows stretched obscenely.

When the gunfire in the area of the bus lessened, *Blueeyes* lifted off me, grabbed my hand, and pulled me into a crouched position, screaming over the noise. "Stay close!"

As we made our way to the rear of the bus, I began to hear the screams, death cries intermixed with gunshots, popping and wailing. The house at the end of the street was engulfed in flames, the one beside it lit along the bottom. A man charged from the front door, back on fire, rifle in hand. He was shooting blindly at everything, screaming as the flames overtook him. A *howler* emerged from the darkness, wrapped its jaws around his midsection, and shook its head until he ripped it in two. It might have been Willie; too dark too tell.

They were dying. All of them were dying. The little girl popped into my head: her red dress, the way she clutched her father's leg. I couldn't shake the image, tried so hard. It wouldn't go away.

The moment we reached the rear of the bus,

something exploded outside. It was close, so close
one half of the gargantuan vehicle took to the air. My
ears popped. Something behind my eyes ruptured. My
feet left the floor. Suddenly I was airborne, tumbling
with the bus, fire cracking around me, smoke clogging
my face. I hit everything, bouncing back and forth in
our rolling tomb. Something smacked my shoulder
and popped it from the joint. My leg twisted, bent in a
way legs aren't meant to bend. When the bus stopped
rolling, the roof was beneath me, embers popping
inches from my face, soot coating my lungs. I opened
my eyes and saw only black and subtle shades of gray
that burnt my face. My head hurt, throbbed. Blood
trickled down the side of my face, into my ear, and
along my neck. I was cut, bleeding from somewhere
under my hair. Instinctively, I rolled to my stomach,
crawling nowhere specific, anywhere at all. When I hit
a wall of fire I turned around. When I found what I
believed to be a window, I climbed through, flipped,
and landed on my back. The smoke was too thick and
I inhaled too much of it. I tried to breathe and
coughed, black mucus spraying from my mouth, eyes
red with tears. For a moment, the smoke parted. It
didn't last, not nearly enough for me to get a sense of
where I was. I could still hear the screams all around
me, punctuated with flurries of gunfire. Someone
cursed, stopped midsentence, and gurgled. I tried to
sit up. My back had other ideas. My legs went limp.
The pain in my shoulder was too much and my arm
crumpled. Another explosion. Gunfire. Flames. A

man yelled.

Blueeyes?

Couldn't tell.

The fire behind me was spreading, slowly overtaking the bus. I could feel it on my back, so hot it hurt. I needed to move. The next time I sat up, I bit my lip so hard it bled. When I tried to stand my leg nearly folded. A flash of pain shot through my arms and down my spine and made friends with the pain already coursing through my back. I ignored it, had to. I needed to move and keep moving. I needed to find *Blueeyes,* needed somewhere to hide. Before I even took a step I heard the growl, so close. Through the smoke its eyes appeared, deep red, ghostly, almost glowing. I froze, praying it didn't see me, that the smoke was too thick, that it couldn't hear me whimper over the noise.

Its eyes narrowed. It took a step forward.

Without thinking, I reached for *Pointycrunch and* lifted him over my shoulder, amazed he was still in one piece. The wind whistled and the smoke thinned for a fraction of a second. White teeth shimmered and reflected hints of fire. The *howler* growled. With an arrow in *Pointycruch,* I fired into the black, aiming for the teeth. I heard it pierce flesh. The growling didn't stop. The monster didn't care. I fired again; it hit. It didn't matter. I was a bug, a nuisance. I was food. The beast screamed so loud the cloud of smoke ruptured and opened wide. For the first time I saw the whole of its face covered in soot, soaked in sweat, snout stained with blood. There was an arrow sticking out of its back, another in its neck. Its head lowered, lips quivered, exposed teeth drooling. Anxious paws scraped pavement, kicking up stone, preparing to attack.

In that moment I knew I was gone. I couldn't fight it. There was nothing I could. *Pointycrunch* couldn't help. *Blueeyes* couldn't save me. I was alone. Everything slowed. I watched the *howler* shake its head and snarl, the mane surrounding its face catching the light. Sweat and blood scattered, without weight. When it moved, the smoke folded around it, embers singeing its face. The beast emerged from the fire with its eyes wide, a force of nature, at one with the world that birthed it. Instead of lowering *Pointycrunch,* I held him forward, stiffened my arms, and straightened my back. I thought of *Blueeyes,* of what he would have wanted from me. I wondered if he was watching. I wanted him to see. Instead of cowering, I fired. The arrow pierced the *howler's* jugular just below the snout, crimson spitting from beneath the fur.

Somehow, its head exploded.

Blood and meat sprayed in every direction, bits of bone peppering my face. The monster's body whipped, jittered violently. What remained of its face froze, mouth locked open, tongue hanging loose. It collapsed in a heap, a crumpled mess of angles and fur.

A hand fell on my shoulder. *Blueeyes* stepped from behind me. His face was filthy with black, half his jacket burnt, the barrel of his shotgun still smoking. His hand moved to my arm, lightly pressing down and lowering my weapon. He nodded.

I knew what it meant.

Blueeyes wrapped his arms around my waist and lifted me into the air. Suddenly, we were running though the smoke and away from the gunfire. Hanging loosely from his side, I listened as the gunfire began to slow, as the explosions stopped. There were no more screams, nothing remotely resembling the sound of a human voice. They had thought they were safe; they had believed it. They were wrong.

They were wrong and they were dead.

When we reached the wall of debris protecting the street, half of it was gone, reduced to rubble by *howler* jaws, destroyed like everything it was meant to protect. We passed through easily, took to the road. Again I thought of the little girl, her mother, and Sam. I imagined her face-to-face with *howler,* helpless with tears in her eyes. I pictured her pretty red dress, now a shade darker. It was an awful thought. It was probably true. A part of me wanted to turn around, go back and help and see if any of them had survived. It was a stupid idea, childish. There was nothing I could do, nothing *Blueeyes* could do. There was nothing anyone could do.

Not anymore.

Blueeyes ran for nearly an hour through darkened streets, unable to see even a foot in front of him. He never put me down. I could hear the *gimps* moaning, hungry voices from the abyss. *Blueeyes* heard them as well and ran in the opposite direction, never stopped moving. We took shelter in a shed, small, roof collapsing. While it wasn't safe, it was the closest thing we could find. The door wouldn't close, so *Blueeyes* held it shut. He remained in that position for some time, one hand holding the door, the other on his gun, struggling to catch his breath and making sure to do it quietly. I watched him, the way his head fell and his eyes closed. He looked so tired, like a man who hadn't slept in years and may never sleep again. He told me to *rest,* that I needed to *lie on my left side* and *stay off my shoulder.* I didn't listen. Instead, I moved beside him, hand on the door as well. It hurt. My arm was in agony. I didn't care. He let go of his gun for just a moment, long enough to wipe the *howler* blood from my face.

I smiled. "Thanks."

He nodded.

I told him what he wanted to hear. "Tomorrow we'll cut my hair."

It was the last thing we said that night.

In the morning, *Blueeyes* checked my shoulder. "Not broken. You're lucky."

When he was done, he cut my hair, trimmed it so short I couldn't feel it on my back or push it up and over my ear. It felt strange, uncomfortable. I didn't feel like myself.

He rubbed the top of my shaved head and grinned in his half-smile sort of way. "Looks good."

I could learn to live with it.

Before we left the shed, I made him cut his beard. "It's too long. Something might grab it."

He agreed. He looked different when the hair was gone. He reminded me of Father. We did our best to avoid packs of *gimps* that day, but occasionally put down a straggler. My leg stopped hurting a few hours later. The pain in my shoulder dulled. While my back was sore, it wasn't sore enough to make me complain. I was alive. That's all that mattered. I spent most of the day playing with my head, running my fingers through what remained of my hair. I couldn't remember ever having short hair; I always liked it long, like Mother.

It was growing on me.

For the most part, the day was uneventful. Afternoon arrived quickly. In no time at all, we found ourselves on the outskirts of town. *Gimp* numbers dwindled. For nearly an hour we saw nothing. With night approaching, we happened on an isolated group of them, five or six, plodding aimlessly from one side of the street to the other, dead eyes in sunken skulls. Half of them looked too worn, too old to be dangerous. Their bodies had decayed to the point that some muscles became useless. They could barely lift their legs, shuffling more than stepping. When I asked *Blueeyes* how long *gimps* lived, he said it *depended on how much they ate.* Eating slowed the decay of their bodies. If they ate regularly they could, potentially, live forever.

When I asked him how long he would live, he ignored me.

Instead of responding, *Blueeyes* ducked behind a nearby car, back to the steel. Instinctively, I followed. We remained there for a minute, hunched in silence.

When he finally spoke, he seemed annoyed. "What are you waiting for?"

I was confused. "What?"

"Target practice. Won't get any better if you don't shoot."

My confusion disappeared, replaced with excitement. We'd spent so much time running and hiding. I hadn't shot *Pointycrunch* in days. I missed him. He missed me. I lifted him from my shoulder and retrieved an arrow from the sack strapped to my back. When I had everything I needed, I moved to the front of the car, extended my arms over the hood, and took aim. Reality set in quickly. I was overanxious. The *gimps* were further away than I thought, further than anything I'd shot. There was no way I could hit them, not from that distance. *Pointycrunch* was disappointed. We were both disappointed.

I relaxed my grip. "They're too far."

Blueeyes' response was predictable. "No, they're not."

"I've never hit anything that far away."

"Exactly."

I wanted to shoot *Blueeyes* and cursed him under my breath. He was wrong. They were way too far.

"Were losing light, Megan."

I really wanted to shoot him.

When I realized we weren't going anywhere until I tried, I relented. Closing one eye, I focused on the tallest and slowest of the group. It was a man, dead flesh peeling from a crumpled skull, wisps of gray hair whipping in the breeze. One of his arms was hanging from his torso. His shoulder was an open wound, useless. With his back to me, I noticed that his neck was twisted at an awkward angle, nearly bent backward. It had to be broken. He was a mess. He was also moving away from me.

My shoulders slumped. "I'll never hit him from here."

"Bow can shoot twice that far. Trust me, I made it. Stop thinking. Do it."

I shook my head, gritted my teeth, and huffed. I wanted to stomp my feet. The look on *Blueeyes'* face wasn't helping matters: so self-assured, as if I was *silly* for doubting him. The muscles in my back tightened. I readjusted my grip and pulled the bowstring back as far as I could, so far I felt it in my shoulder. I followed the movement of the *gimp,* the shuffling of his feet, the bobbing of his skull.

Blueeyes was watching, moving closer. I could feel him over my shoulder, lining up the shot from behind me, breath on my neck. "Shoot where he's going to be, not where he is."

I steadied my arms, held my breath, and fired. The arrow connected with the *gimp's* upper back, jerked him forward, and tossed him to the mud. I missed his head by at least a foot.

I was amazed I hit him at all. "Damn it."

"Watch the language."

Damn it.

Blueeyes handed me another arrow. "Try again."

With the first *gimp* slow to get up, I turned my attention to another. I'm not sure if it was a man or woman. I suppose it didn't matter. It wasn't either anymore. Whatever it was, it was dressed in a trench coat, bottom frayed and faded, filth a decade old. I lifted *Pointycrunch* and readied myself.

Blueeyes' hand fell to my shoulder and slid across my bicep to my elbow. His fingers made adjustments. "Keep your arm straighter."

With his other hand he lifted my head. "Chin up."

My arm was strained, shoulder throbbing. Both of *Blueeyes'* hands fell to my waist, fingers pinched. My back straightened. His voice lowered to a whisper. The inflection was something I'd never heard from him, almost encouraging. "Ignore the distance. Distance doesn't matter. Ugly son of a bitch might as well be five feet away, standing right in front of you. All you have to do is reach out and touch it. Just touch its head. If you don't, you're done for. It won't give you a second chance, Megan. If you miss…you're dead."

I released the arrow. It sliced through air, through flesh, skull, and eye. The *gimp* fell.

Blueeyes handed me another. "Hit the rest and I'll be impressed." He wasn't smiling. He never smiled.

Still, it felt like he was smiling.

I dispatched the next three *gimps* with ease, a single shot for each. One of my arrows entered through one ear and exited the other. I was especially proud of that. By the time the *gimp* I'd hit in the shoulder was back on his feet, I dropped him to the mud. *Blueeyes* was already standing, tightening the straps of his backpack, heading in the opposite direction. Only one *gimp* remained, a woman with her back to me. She looked slightly *fresher* than the rest, long dark hair, blotchy skin mostly intact. I watched her move, the way she shuffled, the gait of her step. I was so anxious for her to turn, so proud of myself for what I'd done that I didn't notice her clothes or the specific tint of her hair. I should have noticed. I certainly wasn't paying attention to the bracelet dangling from her arm. The details were lost, meaningless. In that moment she wasn't even a *her*.

She wasn't a *gimp* and she wasn't a monster. I wasn't scared of her and she couldn't hurt me. She was unimportant, a *thing*. She was target practice. I wanted to kill her.

I wanted to kill her so badly.

The moment she turned, my shoulders dropped. *Pointycrunch* slipped from my fingers, fell to the dirt. Something inside twisted, lurched. A lump of awful, balled and congealed, wedged itself in my throat, refusing to budge. Everything went numb. Everything turned fuzzy. I couldn't breathe. Suddenly, I was crying. Suddenly, I was running. I was running to her.

Blueeyes yelled, screamed. I don't know what he said, didn't care. I could hear him behind me, chasing, boots splashing in the mud. I hopped over a fallen garbage can, through a bit of broken fence, arms pumping, chest heaving. I was less than thirty feet away when she saw me. The lump in my throat erupted, spewed from my mouth as an incoherent gurgle. Our eyes met. She recognized me. I swore she recognized me. I could see it in her eyes. Behind the milky overcast there was *something*. I saw it, felt it. When the tears from my eyes hit my lips, I tasted it. Her arms raised, fingers twiddling. When she opened her mouth her dimples came to life.

Those dimples.

Blueeyes snagged my shirt and held tight. My feet took to the air, suddenly above my head. When I hit the ground, I hit hard. The fall knocked the wind from my lungs and opened a gash on the back of my head. *Blueeyes* was on top of me instantly, struggling to contain my flailing limbs and screaming for me to *stop fighting*. I wanted him off, wanted him away. I balled my hand into a fist and punched his stupid face. I kicked him in the chest so hard I hoped I broke his ribs. I clawed his cheek with my fingers, jabbed my thumb in his eye.

"No! Get off me! Get off!"

When he pinned my arm to the mud, I bit his hand and tasted blood.

"Stop it! God damn it, Megan!"

"No!" When the bite didn't bother him, I kicked his groin. "Let me go!"

No matter what I did or how hard I struggled, *Blueeyes* refused to let go. He was massive and strong, a tower of flesh fighting back, moving with me, always a step ahead. He held my arms, hands full of my clothes. After pinning my legs he maneuvered himself up my body. When he reached my chest I was done for. That's when I saw her over his shoulder, hands reaching for his back, mouth open and head cocked. She was coming to help me.

I truly believed she'd come to help.

Blueeyes sensed her presence the same way he sensed everything. While maintaining his position on my chest he retrieved his knife, turned to face her, and drove the blade into her chest. I screamed so loud I felt it in my chest, in my arms and legs and eyes. I felt it in my heart. When *Blueeyes* lunged at her again I lunged too, snagged his arm, squeezed and pulled. Instead of connecting with her head, he hit her shoulder.

"Damn it, Megan!"

When he tried again, I did the same. The knife slid into her side, black blood spitting from the wound. *Blueeyes* knocked me to the ground and stood from my chest. I locked my arms around his midsection. Hanging from his back, I rammed my head into his spine, scratching anything exposed. When he stumbled backward and landed on top of me, something in my chest cracked. I couldn't breathe. When she came at him again, *Blueeyes* kicked her in the stomach, knocking her to the mud. He tried to stand, but I was still holding on, refusing to let go. I didn't care that I couldn't breathe. It didn't matter that something was broken in my chest. I couldn't let him hurt her. With my legs around his waist, I climbed his back, coiled my arms around his neck, and squeezed. When I dug my elbow into the open wound on his shoulder, he growled.

Blueeyes wanted to hit me. I could tell he wanted to hit me. He probably wanted to kill me. He was cursing, arms flailing, desperately trying to shake me loose and coming up empty. His fingers went for mine, peeling them from the flesh of his neck. By this time she was back on her feet. I could hear her moaning, swiping at *Blueeyes,* clawing his jacket with filthy digits. The instant *Blueeyes* pried me loose I was airborne, weightless, flying over his shoulder. The ground smacked me harder this time. I bit my tongue, tasted blood. My shoulder popped. My left side went numb. Everything blurred, flashed black, then came back again. *Blueeyes* was above me, struggling to keep her from removing a chunk of his neck with her teeth. One of his hands slid down his side, reaching for a second knife strapped to his leg.

"N-no...s-sh—" I opened my mouth, squeaked. He couldn't hear me. I could barely hear myself. My voice was gone, lungs empty, chest on fire. *Blueeyes* retrieved his blade when she latched onto his arm and bit down. He snarled, nostrils flared, eyes wide. He was going to kill her. He was going to kill her *again.*

My mouth exploded. "She's my mother!"

Blueeyes paused, knife in the air, Mother gnawing on his forearm, blood seeping from the corners of her mouth. Instead of stabbing her, he cracked the butt of the weapon against her jaw. The blow knocked her loose, broken teeth spilling from her lips. His foot connected with her knee, shattering bone and bending it backward. She fell forward, face first into the mud, moaning the entire time. *Blueeyes* dropped his weight onto her back, knee to her spine. He snagged a handful of hair, mashed her further into the filth. When he looked at me, he was panting, covered in sweat, Mother flailing beneath him. He seemed furious. He was disappointed. He was sad. Mother's head twisted sideways, caked in mud. Her eyes moved to me, stayed there. When she reached for me, I reached back.

"Megan, don't…"

Her fingers brushed mine, gently violent, distant but familiar—so achingly familiar.

"It's not your mother."

I ignored *Blueeyes*. I didn't care what he thought, cared even less about what he had to say. It was her. It had to be her. I wanted it to be her so badly that it didn't matter that it wasn't, not anymore. The instant our hands met, she grabbed my wrist, twisted, and pulled, held so tight I felt it pop. Her mouth opened, screamed, snapped at my fingers. *Blueeyes* stomped her forearm with his boot. I heard the bones break, an awful snap I'll never forget. She barely noticed. When he stomped again, she finally let go.

Blueeyes pressed his elbow to the back of her head

and shoved her face to the mud, muffling her moans. He looked at me, at my quivering lips, at the tears in my eyes. "Walk away, Megan."

The thing I once called Mother wiggled her head free for the briefest of moments, long enough to growl. Her face was coated in filth, eyes wild, decaying fingers clawing at dirt. That's when I noticed her cheeks, sunken and gray, skin blotched and peeling. Her features had changed so much. Her dimples were gone, swallowed by receding flesh, erased. She wasn't my mother. My mother was dead. My mother died on the side of the road, shivering and alone with whatever disease had eaten her insides. My mother wasn't coming back.

Nothing ever comes back, even when it does.

"Megan…go." *Blueeyes'* voice was softer than I'd ever heard it. "Grab your things and head for the road. Don't turn around. Don't look back. I'll meet you there."

I knew what he was going to do and why he wanted me to walk away. I knew it and I didn't try to stop him. It was difficult to stand, more difficult to walk. My back was throbbing, shoulder on fire. Everything hurt. Everything was torn, ripped to pieces and scattered in the dirt. I was broken inside and out. I'd walked less than twenty feet when I heard the knife break her skull and pierce her brain. She stopped moaning.

It was over.

Blueeyes stayed close to me for the remainder of the day. We didn't speak. There wasn't anything to say. I watched the sun and the clouds, staring through tear-soaked eyes. When the moon emerged, I watched it, too. The sky was clear that night, the clearest I'd seen in years, so clear I could see the stars. Mother once said the stars weren't really there, that they were *light fifty years old, ghosts.* I hated when she told me that. I didn't like that at all.

Blueeyes found a suitable shelter shortly after the sun disappeared and everything went black. It was a large building, high ceilings, with broken furniture littering the floor. Hanging in the center of the room was a massive glass structure, hundreds of delicately carved bits dangling from the underside and shimmering in the moonlight. The steel holding the whole thing together was weathered and bent, barely hanging on and coated in a layer of dust a decade thick. I imagined what it must have looked like before I was born, probably beautiful. I didn't understand it. It didn't make sense. It seemed silly for something so elaborate to exist without a purpose, to create something so lavish and let it rot away. I hated it.

We settled into a much smaller room deeper into the structure and off the beaten path. The door was solid, the lock sturdy. We were safe there. I slid down a wall on the far end, pulled my knees to my chest, and buried my face between them. I wanted to sleep. I wanted to sleep so bad. Didn't care if I woke. I was surprised when *Blueeyes* sat beside me, even more when he grabbed my hand.

What happened next surprised me the most.

"I'm sorry, Megan."

His thumb moved lightly over the top of my hand, back and forth, skin surprisingly soft. He sighed, working up the nerve to speak. "After those things…they did what they did to my little girl…after I realized I wasn't dead and the moans died down…" His voice was a whisper, breathy and uneven. "I left my little hiding place…went back into the living room."

He paused, squeezed my hand. "She was still there, still *alive*. Megan…my little Megan…" His voice cracked, snapped in two. "Those bastards…they ate everything but her head. They turned her into one of them and left her there…screaming."

I lifted my head and looked at *Blueeyes*. He was staring at the ceiling, at the shadows and the black, expressionless. I heard him inhale, felt it in the air. When he closed his eyes, I shivered. When he squeezed my hand again, I squeezed back.

"You don't remember what it was like before all this bullshit, Megan. Be thankful for that. It wasn't perfect, but it wasn't this. We were violent, and stupid, and silly, but we were something. We had a chance. There were possibilities. You were born here…nothing to hold on to. There's nothing tethering you to all the wasted-*fucking*-potential.

At the time, I didn't know what he meant. It didn't matter. I liked having him next to me, talking the way he was talking. I liked listening to him, his voice. I liked the way his hand felt, liked holding it. We remained in that exact position, hand-in-hand, until morning. At some point during the night I drifted off. When I woke a few hours later, *Blueeyes* was still beside me, staring straight ahead. It was too dark to be certain, but his eyes seemed red and puffy, as if he'd been crying. When he felt me move he looked away. That night he never let go of my hand. Not once. Not for a minute.

It was perfect, the last perfect moment of my life.

16

Morning arrived the same as always. We gathered
our things, bandaged my hand, and took to the road.
The clouds moved in quickly, dark and thick,
blanketing the sky. By midday the sun was a memory.
Despite my injuries we were making good time;
hadn't seen a *gimp* all day. It was quiet, chilly. The
breeze felt good on my face, and the temperature
numbed the ache in my hand. *Blueeyes* said it wasn't
broken, maybe fractured, maybe just sprained. He
spent the morning apologizing to me anyway. There
was something different about him, softer, more
approachable. I made a joke about his terrible
bandage job and I think he even smiled. As we
walked, he would occasionally check on me.

"How you doing back there?"

"Feeling okay?"

"Doing alright, kiddo?"

He'd never called me *kiddo* before, no one had. I liked it. I started calling myself *kiddo* in my head, imagined other people saying it to me, shaking hands with someone and introducing myself as *kiddo*. It was silly. It felt good to be silly.

The farther we walked, the larger the surrounding structures became. One-story houses transformed to two-story buildings. Two-story buildings turned into eight-floor apartments. The forest tapered off, replaced by cracked concrete and weathered blacktop. The road became congested, littered with husks of burnt vehicles, haphazardly constructed roadblocks older than I was.

I poked *Blueeyes* in the back. "Where are we going?"

"The city."

I'm not sure why I asked him. I already knew the answer, I just couldn't believe it. My entire life I'd avoided cities. *Father* said they were dangerous, overrun with *gimps* and *biters* and the sort of people that couldn't be trusted. I didn't want to go to the city or anywhere near the city. It felt wrong.

I poked my friend again, tugged on his jacket. "Why?"

"I left something there. It's important. I need to get it back."

"What is it?"

"Something important."

"Why is it so important?"

Blueeyes sighed. "It just is."

"But why?"

He sighed again. "You ask way too many questions, Megan. Just trust me. I'm guessing Travis and his people don't make their way into the city too often. The more distance we can put between us and that asshole the better."

Bloodboots. I kept forgetting about *Bloodboots.*

I waited a few minutes before bothering *Blueeyes* again. "I thought the cities were dangerous."

"They are."

"Then why...I mean…why are we…"

He turned to face me, dropped to one knee, and put his hands on my shoulders. Strangely, being eye level with him made me feel better. He probably knew it would. "We'll be alright. Trust me. I spent more time in that city than I ever should have. I know my way around." He squeezed my shoulder in a reassuring way, placed his hand on my cheek, and patted gently. He probably knew I would like that, too.

I stopped asking questions.

A few hours later, buildings began to rise from the horizon, massive things, dark silhouettes against a sky of gray. I'd never seen anything like it, so many of them in one place, an ocean of steel and stone, burnt and crumbling. It seemed to go on forever. We were so close, just miles away. If we kept moving this way, we would reach it by nightfall. My feet stopped moving. My eyes stopped blinking. I really didn't want to go to the city.

When *Blueeyes* realized I wasn't keeping pace, he chuckled. "Don't tell me you've never seen a city."

I shook my head. "Not this close."

My eyes moved to a single building rising above the rest, so impossibly tall the clouds swallowed the top. My lips felt dry, head heavy. I might have taken a step backward.

"Listen, Megan, there's no—" The sky roared, lightning flashed. *Blueeyes* looked up. "Damn it."

He scanned the surrounding area, settled on a small row of buildings a few hundred yards in the opposite direction, and pointed. "Looks like you won't have to worry about the city until tomorrow. We'll wait out the storm over there, leave first thing in the morning."

I didn't argue.

By the time we reached the buildings, the rain was falling: a soft drizzle, the calm before the storm. The area was a mess: *gimp* corpses everywhere, upturned cars, collapsed walls reduced to piles of rubble. The place looked different than it had from a distance. The closer we moved, the more I realized something was wrong. I'd seen rubble. I'd seen dead *gimps* and destroyed buildings before. I'd seen a lot of them. There was something very *fresh* about the way everything was laid out, as if the dust had just settled.

Blueeyes noticed it too. His hand fell to my chest. "Wait."

He moved away from me, softly stepping up to a *gimp* corpse a few feet away. Once there, he dropped to one knee, reached forward, and rolled it onto its back. His finger instantly went to the hole in its head and to the spatter of bullets in its chest. He poked and pulled back blood. That's when I smelled the smoke.

Blueeyes smelled it, too. "We're getting ou—"

I heard the gunshot before I saw his knee explode. Blood sprayed from his leg, erupting in every direction, chunks of bone sent skyward. *Blueeyes'* leg folded backward, cracked, and bent in a way legs aren't meant to bend. When he hit the dirt, he snarled.

"Get down, Megan!" Screaming through his teeth, he lunged forward, snagged the fabric of my pants, and dragged me to the dirt.

Another gunshot. The ground beside us split, stone and sand. *Blueeyes* crawled on top of me as the gunfire increased, pelting the surrounding area in rapid succession, ricocheting off steel, mauling earth. His back ruptured in two places. His arm tore open. With his arms around me, we rolled across the dirt and behind a nearby car. A volley of gunfire pelted the frame, shattered the windshield, and flattened a tire. *Blueeyes* was already reaching for his shotgun, struggling to load it, hands slippery with blood.

"*Fuckgoddamnitfucksostupidsostupid.*" He was talking to himself, growling under his breath, cursing through gritted teeth.

His hand went to my head and shoved me face first to the dirt. "Stay down!"

He rose for a second, fired through the shattered

windshield, ducked momentarily, and fired again. Everything was happening too fast, too loud, too much all at once. *Blueeyes* fired again. A spray of bullets crisscrossed the hood of the car, tearing it to pieces, gunfire ringing in my ears. Above me, a headlight exploded. Bits of glass scattered across my hair. Through half closed eyes I peeked at my friend; his chest was soaked in blood, his neck painted red. A chunk of his hand was missing. His fingers wouldn't work. While trying to reload, he dropped his gun. I needed to help him, needed to do something more than what I was doing. Reaching over my shoulder, I grabbed *Pointycrunch,* tore him from my back, and loaded an arrow.

Blueeyes noticed what I was doing, knocked him from my hands, and shoved me to the ground. "Damn it! Stay down!"

Something hit his chest, sprayed his face with blood, and tossed him backward violently. His eyes closed, face contorted. His hands went to his chest, crimson pouring through the cracks in his fingers. Without thinking I retrieved *Pointycrunch,* rose above the hood of the car, and let loose. It was a blind shot, a silly shot. I didn't know what I was aiming at, maybe nothing. The gunfire continued, tore the bumper from the car, and lifted a section of steel from the side. It was everywhere, all at once. A cloud of dust and bits of shrapnel rose around us. I could taste it; I swallowed it. It coated my throat and wormed its way into the spaces between my eyes and up my nose. Instead of breathing, I coughed. Blindly, I grabbed another arrow, loaded, and fired again. I barely felt the bullet that tore open my shoulder, at least at first. The impact knocked me back and deposited me in the dirt beside *Blueeyes*. The pain came all at once, so much that I thought I was dead. I had to be dead. It spread quickly across my shoulder, down my side, and into my legs. When I tried to move, I couldn't. My lower half locked, froze in place. Instinctively, my hand went to the wound and pressed into mushy flesh, warm blood trickling down my arm. I screamed and cursed louder than I'd ever screamed or cursed, so loud the words transformed into something guttural, animalistic. I wasn't myself anymore. I was a wounded animal, target practice.

When *Blueeyes* rolled toward me, a pair of arms wrapped around his neck, massive and muscular, skin like dark steel. Another set of hands snagged his arm. A third wrestled the shotgun from his hand. Suddenly, he was airborne, thrown to the dirt, pulled in the opposite direction, and slammed roughly. Someone stomped his leg and cracked the side of his face with the butt of a rifle.

"No!" When I reached for him someone else grabbed my arm. Fingers clutched my hair and tugged violently, tearing it from my scalp in clumps. Arms coiled around my waist, lifting. My feet left the ground and a shoe feel off. I kicked, wiggled, and reached behind me with my good arm, scratching at whoever had me. The more I struggled, the tighter he squeezed. I couldn't breathe. Someone punched me in the stomach and laughed when I belched blood. A random hand emerged from nowhere and smacked my head so hard the world began to spin. Everything twisted and bent, blurred. I was surrounded. A sea of men converged, filthy hands grabbing my legs, pawing my chest, and pulling at my clothes. There were so many of them, so many angry faces and leering grins. When someone poked my wounded shoulder, I bit so hard I nearly swallowed my tongue.

"Calm down, princess! Calm down!"

At first I didn't recognize the voice, hard to discern among the men. The noises mashed together in such a way that this one was without distinctiveness. Everything was one. One made no sense.

A hand covered my mouth, clamped tight, and pulled my head back. I felt his lips near my ear, inches away, acid breath on my neck. "I told you I was going to hurt you, Megan; told you it couldn't be helped."

Bloodboots. He found us.

His face touched mine, cheek-to-cheek, scratchy

stubble against my skin. The sea of cackling men parted and I spotted *Blueeyes*. He was twenty feet away, on his knees in the dirt. Two men held him firmly, stretching his arms in opposite directions while another choked him from behind. A boot kicked his stomach. A fist punched his face so hard bloody teeth hit dirt.

It was instinct alone that caused me to bite *Bloodboots'* palm. I dug my teeth deep through sweat and flesh until I tasted blood. When his hand moved away I screamed. "*Nonononono*! Stop! Please stop!"

Instead of stopping, they hit *Blueeyes* harder. The group swarmed, hands punching, legs kicking: a wall of all consuming violence. In the group I recognized *Scarface,* grinning as he hammered my friend, face contorted in such a way he hardly looked human.

The voice of *Bloodboots* stabbed my ear. "You want them to stop, princess?"

I nodded, overcome with emotions and unable to speak, choked with tears.

"You want me to tell them to leave him alone? They'll listen to me. Those are my men, my *monsters.* If I tell them to stop, they'll stop."

It was awful, the sound of flesh on flesh, blood-wet, cracking knuckles. It wouldn't stop. I would have done anything to make it stop.

Bloodboots was unrelenting. "Ask me. Ask me to tell them to leave him alone."

I couldn't speak, couldn't think, and couldn't look away. When I closed my eyes, I still heard it. They were killing him. *Blueeyes* was dying. He was dying and there was nothing I could do to help him. They were going to make me watch.

What emerged from my mouth was incomprehensible, a gurgle and a scream, something without definition. "*S-s-stop top-stop-op!*"

Bloodboots snickered. "Come on, you can do better than that. Ask me nice. Say, *please.*"

"*Ple-pea-se-leasplease!*"

It wasn't a word, just sounds and nothing more, desperate pleading from someone with nothing left. It was all I had to offer.

Bloodboots snickered. His mouth moved from my ear. "You heard the little princess, you sons of bitches! Step away from the man!"

I'm not sure how I managed to lift my head, not sure how I even moved. Everything was limp, rubbery. My head weighed a thousand pounds, neck useless. Whatever fight I had left in me was gone. Through teary eyes I watched as the mass of flesh parted, slowly, one-by-one, laughing between labored breaths. When they were gone, there was only *Blueeyes*. His head hung loosely on his neck, chin resting on his chest. He remained upright because it's what the men holding his arms wanted. If they'd let him go he would have crumpled. Every part of him was puffy, blue and purple, ripped to pieces and drenched in blood.

When I tried to talk, *Bloodboots* covered my mouth. "Shhh." I didn't bite him, didn't even try. I just cried. *Blueeyes* looked at me lazily through blood-clumped hair, his face a mess of mauled flesh. I cried even more.

Bloodboots chuckled. "You're one *tough* motherfucker, aren't you?" He was talking to *Blueeyes* now, watching as my friend struggled to meet his gaze, body racked with pain. "Help him out, Darrell. I want him to look at me when I'm talking to him."

Scarface moved behind *Blueeyes,* snagged a handful of his hair, and pulled his head back. I could almost *feel Bloodboots* smile. I didn't need to see his face to confirm it.

Maintaining his grip on my waist, he moved us closer to my fallen friend. "You're the one who let the *howlers* loose, aren't you? Just to rescues this bitch?" His arms tightened, fingers digging roughly into my flesh. "What are you, her *daddy?* Is this your *daddy,* sweetie? Are we hurting your *daddy?*"

When I didn't answer, he squeezed tighter, mashed his chin against the hole in my shoulder. I yelped, kicked, and wiggled, which accomplished nothing. Even in his beaten haze, *Blueeyes* heard me screaming. When he reacted, the beating began again.

"Someone hold this brat for me!"

Two men pried me from *Bloodboots'* arms and stretched me horizontally, cackling through unkempt whiskers. The man holding my upper half brought me to his face, licked my cheek, then licked his lips and smiled so *goddamn* ugly. The moment *Bloodboots* took a step toward *Blueeyes,* the crowd stopped punching, parted, and let him through.

The leader of the mob dropped to one knee, reached forward, and lifted the beaten face of my friend. His voice went cold, changed into something deadly serious, every word punctuated by anger. "My friends died when you did that, lots of them. My little brother died when you did that. But you didn't think about that, did you? You didn't care about my little brother. You didn't give a shit." He moved his head closer, eyes narrowing. "All for this stupid little girl. My brother died for a worthless little bitch."

Blueeyes' head jerked and his jittery lips parted, his unsteady gaze settling on the man kneeling before him. His voice was nearly a whisper. It was all he could muster, all he needed. "Touch the girl and I'll kill you."

"Excuse me?"

Blood poured from a gash on his head and over his nose, mouth and chin. When he spoke, he spit, scarlet venom. "You heard me."

Bloodboots shook his head, then grinned. "You're serious, aren't you? Your face is a fucking mess, you're missing half your hand, you've got three, maybe four bullets in you, and you're threatening me?" He laughed out loud. "You don't win, stupid. You aren't walking away from this."

He moved even closer to *Blueeyes'* face, barely an inch between them. "Don't worry though, I'm not going to *touch* the girl. Not really my thing." With a hand, he motioned to the group. "*They're* going to hurt her though. By the time these *sickos* are done with her she'll beg me to put her out of her misery, and I'll give her what she wants. Don't worry, we won't make her dinner. She won't be touching my lips. She's not worth it. You know what I will do, though? No? No ideas? You're going to love this. The moment she turns into a *gimp,* or a *biter,* or whatever the hell she's going to be, I'm going to kill her again. This one's going to die twice and I'm going to enjoy every...*fucking*...minute."

Blueeyes' hands turned to fists. His face went

black. When he screamed, he snarled. His hand shot forward, fingers snapping at *Bloodboots'* neck, teeth chomping, eyes wide.

"Kill yo—" The butt of a rifle put an end to his attack, cracked his skull, and planted him face-first in the mud. When that didn't knock him out, it cracked again. On cue the crowd swarmed, vicious, attacking with disturbing glee. They beat him for a solid minute, smacking him with steel, stomping on his head, and stabbing his back. When the knives weren't enough to hold him down, they began to put bullets his back. They were mauling him. At some point I closed my eyes. If my hands hadn't been pinned to my sides I would have covered my ears. If I'd had a knife of my own I would have cut my ears off.

The abuse didn't stop until *Bloodboots* ordered it to stop. "Alright, alright, alright! That's just about enough, gentlemen. Back off! Give the man some room!" He looked at me and grinned. He was in charge. He was in control. He wanted me to know that.

The huffing crowd retreated, forming a semi-circle around their plaything, clothes spattered crimson, breathing ragged and ready. At the center of the group was what remained of my friend, painted red, sticky, and puffy. He wasn't a man anymore. He was a broken *thing,* a lump of meat with a heart. A section of flesh covering his skull had peeled away and folded over, an awful wet slab flapping in the breeze. Somehow, despite everything they'd done to him, *Blueeyes* moved. His back creaked, lurched, and bent into a shape vaguely resembling straight. I'm not sure if he even knew I was there, if he could hear me crying, begging him to stay down. He wouldn't have listened anyway.

Bloodboots sighed, scratched his head, ran his fingers through his hair, and mumbled under his breath. "You've got to be kidding me."

He watched as *Blueeyes* continued to stir, limbs bent and broken, open wounds breathing the diseased air of a world gone mad. Head bobbing loosely on his neck, he tried to speak and failed, choking on blood. When he finished spitting out his insides, he tried again.

His eyes moved lazily to *Bloodboots* and remained there, impossibly steady. "G-go-gonna ki-il-kill you la-last."

"Motherfuck…" *Bloodboots* had enough and reached for the gun hanging on his hip. He retrieved it from the holster and aimed. I heard it click, heard the round slide into the chamber.

I'll never forget that sound.

In the moment before *Bloodboots* fired, *Blueeyes* looked to me. He wasn't sad or angry; he wasn't fighting back. He knew it was coming and there was nothing he could do. What little remained of his voice cracked. "Cl-close your ey-eyes." I could swear I saw him grin.

I did as he asked.

I heard the shots, two of them, probably aimed at his head. *Bloodboots* laughed. The rest joined in. Someone cheered. There were more shots after that, insult added to injury. I stopped counting. It was a party, the highlight of the day, the joyous signaling of more to come. They enjoyed every minute of it.

And just like that, my friend was gone.

17

I'm not entirely sure when I passed out. At some point I just went to sleep. Unconsciousness rolled in, enveloped me, and carried me away. When *Blueeyes* died everything went fuzzy and distant, the reflected memories of someone else. I didn't care anymore. *Blueeyes* was gone, along with Mother and Father. The only people I'd ever loved, all of them were gone. I remember being tied, legs bound, arms behind my back. I remember the smiles, the cackling, dry lips and rotted teeth, faces caked in filth. I remember seeing *Pointycrunch*, watching him as they carried me away, losing another friend. There was a truck; they tossed me in the back, stuffed between slimy bags packed with unknown meat, an unbearable stench. There

were flies crawling on my face, swarming the bags—
so many flies.

"Too late to head back. We'll hole up for the
night at that place you noticed on the way up." It was
Bloodboots. "No one touches the kid until I have a talk
with her, understand?"

I wasn't looking forward to that.

The drive felt short. I remember wishing it was
longer. I knew what was coming, knew what awaited
me when we came to a stop. I wanted to drive
forever.

The door of the truck swung open. A massive
hand smacked my face. "Wake up." When I didn't
respond it smacked me again.

Scarface pulled me from between the bags of meat
and tossed me over his shoulder. A soft drizzle tickled
my face. Lightning cracked. The clouds lit up. A
storm was growing, the sky angry. The clouds
devoured what remained of the falling sun. All that
was left was a glimmer, obscured by the silhouette of
unfamiliar buildings. The air smelled like sulfur,
burning things I couldn't quite place. Things I wanted
nothing to do with. *Scarface* lugged me through a
doorway and into a dimly lit room with high ceilings
and concrete floors. There were small fires scattered
around the interior, emptied bags and cooking meat.

The area was constructed in a hurry. Nothing seemed finished; everything was unorganized. The smell was awful. As we moved further inside the men watched, toothless grins cast in dancing shadows. Their eyes followed intently, unblinking. I watched them swallow, lick their lips, and grin in a way that sent shivers along my spine.

At the end of the room we moved through another doorway into something smaller and tucked away, a fresh fire snapping in the corner. *Scarface* dropped me to the floor and mumbled something under his breath. When he left he slammed the door so hard it rattled the walls and knocked a lamp from a nearby desk. A lock clicked, then clicked again. I was back where I started: different place, same exact situation. After everything I'd seen, everywhere I'd gone, and everything I'd done, nothing had changed. I was with the same people, the people who stole my father. There was nothing I could do about it. I laid there for some time, face to the floor, cold against my cheek. Outside the storm picked up. I could hear the rain beating against steel, lightning popped, thunder roared. Unlike before, I didn't cry, struggle or squirm. It didn't matter. Wouldn't have made a difference. Struggling accomplished nothing. Father struggled for years to keep us alive, moving, searching for a place that didn't exist. Mother struggled to keep us together and sane. *Blueeyes* struggled until the very end, until they beat him, and shot him, and took him from me.

Struggling was pointless. I was done struggling. Whatever *Bloodboots* was going to do to me, I wanted him to do. I wanted to be done with it all. It was the only way out.

When *Bloodboots* entered the room he shook his head, slid onto the desk beside me, and sighed. "Back where we started, huh, princess?"

I didn't respond, so he kicked me with his foot, making sure to hit my injured shoulder. "I wanted to talk to you before they get their hands on you...won't be much left after that."

I could hear his fingers drumming against the table, a slow, steady beat. "You remind me of someone I used to know. You look like her." His fingers stopped. "I think it's the eyes."

I was already sick of hearing him talk, his voice like nails. Why wouldn't he shut up? I wanted it done, gone.

Get on with it.

"I bet you think I'm a really bad guy, don't you?"

Please shut up.

"This may be difficult for you to understand, considering the position in which you currently find yourself, but I'm not a bad guy...not at all. I'm the good guy, sweetie."

Shut up. Shut up.

"I'm the righteous one. I'm the one righting the wrong. I'm the one avenging a death, not you."

Shut up. Shut up. Shut up. Shut up.

"You and your *daddy*—you hurt my family, hurt me. You took my brother...fed him to those things...turned him into *howler* shit. Patrick was the only thing I had left, the last good person in this fucked-up place, and you killed him. You did that, not me. You and your *daddy*...you did this to yourselves. You left me alone. Whatever happens from this point on is your own fault."

"He wasn't my *daddy.*" I don't know why I said it, why I felt the need or thought it mattered. The words just happened.

"Oh, no?" *Bloodboots* seemed surprised. "Could have sworn I saw a family resemblance. What was he then? A friend? Something more, maybe?" He paused, leaning back, scratching his chin. "Oh, I get it." His voice lowered to a whisper, lips stretched to a grin. "Did I kill your *boyfriend,* sweetie?"

He said it with malice. While he was going to let the rest of them hurt me with their hands, he wanted to do it with his words. He wanted me to cry, wanted tears. For whatever reason, he needed me broken.

"I did, didn't I? I killed your *sweetheart.*" In a single movement he slid from the desk, dropped to his knees, and knelt beside me. "I broke his face, made him bleed…rubbed that fat nose of his right in the dirt. I punched him, and I kicked him, and put a bullet right in his *pervert* head."

Reaching forward, he made his hand into the shape of gun, pressed a finger to my temple, and held it there. "When you really take a moment to think about it, in some ways…I probably did you a favor."

Something in me was boiling, something in my belly. I could feel it splashing, rising, anxiously spitting. It wanted something, anything. It needed everything. It had no interest in going quietly. The next time *Bloodboots* spoke, it snarled.

"The things he did to you he shouldn't have done. He was *sick* man, *sick* in the head. I put him out of his misery, *kiddo.* I di—"

I bit his nose.

I bit until my jaw clamped shut, until tooth cracked tooth, until blood filled my mouth and drenched my eyes. I bit and pulled, tore it from his face. Before spitting it to the floor I held it in my mouth and chewed.

"*Shutupshutupshutsupshutupshutup!*" When I started screaming I didn't stop, the same words, an endless loop, so loud I thought my chest would burst.

Bloodboots staggered to the opposite end of the room, hands covering his nose, face painted red, blood spraying through wobbly fingers. When *Scarface* entered the room I was wailing in *Bloodboots'* direction, eyes wide, legs kicking as I twitched on the floor.

He looked right at me. "What the fu—"

Bloodboots snagged his jacket and tugged, whipping the larger man from side to side as his nose spurted in every direction. "Bitch bit me! Fucking bitch bit me!"

I screamed louder, impossibly loud. I wanted to break their ears. I wanted to collapse the ceiling and explode the sun. Suddenly, I was crawling in their direction, moaning like a hungry *howler,* biting the air like a flesh-starved *gimp.* I'd only eaten a nose. I was hungry for a face. When *Scarface* kicked me in the stomach, I didn't stop. When he stomped my shoulder, I screamed louder. Instead of attacking, *Bloodboots* watched.

Instead of moving forward, he stepped back.

I didn't stop screaming until I heard the explosion: something large, outside, the roof shook and thunder clapped. Gunfire followed, angry voices, confused orders.

"God damn it!" *Scarface* turned from me and headed for the door.

When he opened it, I saw fire. A wall of flames rose from the far side of the building, fiery tendrils arching to the ceiling. Something else exploded. Someone screamed. Without warning a spatter of bullets erupted from *Scarface's* back, meaty chunks spraying the floor and soaking the walls. The massive man stumbled backward, tripped over his own feet, and crashed to his back. With his last breath he looked right at me, eyes wide, as if he couldn't believe he'd been shot. He froze in that position, a dead stare. He never looked away.

A grouping of bullets pattered the floor beside his face and up the wall and into the ceiling. A wall panel tore in two and tumbled to the floor. Outside the room the screams continued. The shape of a man ran past the open doorway, arms flailing, body engulfed in flame. He shrieked and didn't stop, hands on his face, fingers clawing desperately at cooking flesh. Before he hit the ground he hit a wall, engulfed in everything awful, insides crackling. With his back to the wall, *Bloodboots* fumbled with his gun, struggling to load it, mumbling nonsense and spitting blood. Through the open door I watched as another man tumbled to the floor, riddled with bullets from an unknown source. An engine started, then quickly died. The flames in the other room were spreading quickly, moving outward, hungrily searching for more.

Bloodboots finally managed to slide a clip into the chamber of his gun. "Mess with me? Motherfuckers wanna mess with me?" He was babbling, breath ragged and lip quivering.

Another explosion tore through the building and decimated a section of the wall opposite our door. Crumbling stone tumbled to the fire, debris scattering flames. *Bloodboots* closed his eyes, desperately searching for the nerve to act, to do something other than what he was doing.

He looked at me, back at the door and back to me. "*Fuckfuckfuck!*" Halfway through his obscenity his voice cracked, drenched in frustration.

Sliding across the floor he positioned himself alongside the open door, pulled the gun to his face. When he made the mistake of trying to breath though the hole in his face, he choked, cussed and smacked the wall with the back of his hand. After a deep breath through his mouth and a moment to collect himself, he peeked around the corner. Bullets immediately tore the frame to bits, snapping wood, splinters airborne.

Bloodboots hit the wall again, tiny bits of wood embedded in his face. "Goddammit!"

"Give me the girl!"

We recognized the voice, both of us. Neither believed it.

Bloodboots froze. His eyes moved to me. His mouth began to formulate a word, but ultimately said nothing.

"Give me the girl and I'll make it quick."

Through the door I saw only fire, dancing embers, and smoky debris. I knew he was there, my only friend, hidden in the fury of it all, camouflaged by rage. My *monster* had come back.

My *monsters* were worse than his.

Bloodboots scurried across the concrete on his hands and knees. Using the knife hanging from his belt, he cut the rope binding my feet and whipped me into a standing position. "Get up! Get the fuck up!"

He positioned himself behind me, pressed the steel of his gun against my temple, and pushed forward so hard I thought my neck would snap. "I'm coming out, *motherfucker!* Put down your god damn gun or I'll paint the wall with this bitch's brains!"

There was no response.

"Do you hear me? You hear me, you *sonofabitch?* You better *fucking* answer! You better *fucking* answer or I swe—"

"The gun is down!"

Wind whistled. Fire cracked. Outside our fiery tomb, thunder roared. *Bloodboots* wrapped his hand around the back of my neck and squeezed, pinching flesh, nudging me forward. The heat hit my face the instant we stepped from our little room. Most of the building was engulfed, more being devoured by the second. Soon there would be no building left, only fire and the charred remains of what had been. Bodies were scattered everywhere, some set ablaze, others submerged in pools of crimson. There was no sign of my *monster*, only the aftermath of his anger.

Bloodboots pressed the nozzle forward even farther, bending my head so far it touched my shoulder. "Come out, you piece of shit! Get your ass out here or I end her!"

Across from us the flames parted, black smoke spread, and *Blueeyes* emerged. His body was painted gray and red, a sticky mush of blood and soot. He moved, taught muscles stretched to their limit, on the brink of a collapse he refused to allow. The hem of his pant leg seemed to be on fire. He didn't care. There was a hole in his head, a black nothing leading nowhere. He didn't care about that either. *Blueeyes* dropped his weapons, oversized things stolen from the men who tried to take him from me. His hands stretched out. His eyes moved to mine, scanning my face to see what they'd done.

When he spoke, he breathed fire. "Give her to me."

"Y-you, you're n-not…" *Bloodboots* stuttered, stopped and stuttered again.

Blueeyes took a single step forward. "I won't ask again."

The grip on my neck tightened, pinching so hard I felt it in my legs. "I k-killed…we kill…"

Bloodboots' arms went shaky, jittery finger anxiously tracing the trigger of his gun. "Y-you can't be, y-you…"

That's when I knew he wasn't going to let me go. He would have never given me up, not to *Blueeyes,* not to the walking corpse who'd taken everything from him. He was the *good guy*, said so himself. He was going to kill me. He was *always* going to kill me. He needed me dead.

I don't know why I did it or how I even conceived the idea. My body simply moved, independent of rational thought. I didn't consider, didn't plan. It was as an act of desperation, a physical response to a physical situation. As *Bloodboots* babbled through blood-soaked lips at the ghost in the flames, I slid my hands to his leg and coiled my fingers around his knife.

Blueeyes noticed, screamed. "Megan, no!"

He probably had a plan, knew what he was going to do all along. I changed it. I didn't care. When I stabbed *Bloodboots'* leg it was with my full body, a single, fluid motion. If *Blueeyes* hadn't been so angry, he would have been proud. The blade tore through fabric and ripped through flesh, digging into muscle. When I felt it hit bone, I twisted.

Exactly as I was taught.

Bloodboots wailed. The gun fired, so close to my ear. My knees buckled. Sound went away, disappeared. The fire vanished and *Bloodboots* evaporated. In the blink of an eye everything transformed to nothing, replaced by a high-pitch wail, ear-splitting, rattling my brain. When I hit the ground I refused to stay down; I stumbled forward and regained my balance. I had to move, keep moving. I had to get to *Blueeyes*. My friend was charging in my direction, arms outstretched, screaming and pointing. To this day I'm not sure what he said, couldn't hear the words, couldn't hear anything. In the end, I suppose it doesn't matter. I was nearly to him, inches away, when I felt it in my back. Two more steps, just two more steps and he would have had me.

Two more steps and everything would have been different.

My chest opened when the bullet passed through and belched blood, spraying *Blueeyes'* face. He caught me before I hit the ground, collected and pulled me close. I collapsed into his arms, limbs gone, everything numb and fading. I think there was another bullet; not sure where it hit. There was no pain. Nothing hurt anymore. The world changed rapidly into something without form or shape, a *thing* without name. Suddenly, I had no legs. My arms seemed silly. I watched as *Blueeyes* lowered me to the ground, staring at his face. Another bullet hit his shoulder, exploded in slow motion, droplets of blood floating, reflected fire glimmering along an impossibly smooth surface. Another bullet and his arm opened up, brilliant colors, unlike anything I'd seen. He didn't seem to notice. I watched his face contort in a way I didn't think possible, breaking before my eyes. In that moment he was someone else: Father and Mother, everything I loved. Tears emerged from the corners of his eyes, glistening dots the color of his eyes. They stretched, expanded, and rolled across his cheeks, clearing the filth and leaving tracks of flesh.

I watched him cry.

Face still twisted, *Blueeyes* looked away, lowered me to the floor gently, and screamed at *Bloodboots*. Somehow I heard what came next. I shouldn't have, as far away as I was. *Bloodboots* squealed, cried, and begged. When he thought he was done screaming, he screamed some more. *Blueyees* didn't take his time. He also wasn't in a hurry.

When the end finally came, I died alone, the same as Mother and Father, the same as everyone.

Everyone but my friend.

18

It's a strange thing, waking up from death. *Waking up* isn't exactly the way to describe it, more like being born again. It didn't just happen. I wasn't *dead* one minute and *not dead* the next. There was a process. It took a while; it hurt. There are vague images, things I can sort of remember as the change took place. And yet, they aren't real. They aren't *memories,* not as I knew them to be, more like half-happened dreams, the visions of someone other than myself looking down from above. At first, at least, I was an observer. There was a forest, freezing rain and thunder, the wail of *howlers* drawn to the inferno *Blueeyes* left behind. We moved through it quickly, branches like crinkly fingers, reaching and scratching.

I watched *Blueeyes,* defeated and distant, sadness etched into the wrinkles on his face. For a long while I was weightless in his arms, moving among the trees, battered by the rain I couldn't feel. He walked for hours through the night, into the morning, and to night again. He was injured, bleeding with every step. He had to be tired. He never stopped moving. All the while I felt it growing inside me, this *thing* I was becoming. It began in my head and stretched itself along my face, spreading just below my skin. There was pain, so much pain. It was everywhere. I screamed without a mouth, shrieked into the abyss only to have it echo back. It didn't care. This new *thing* felt dark, cold, and sharp like glass. It wanted every part of me. It didn't matter if it had to hurt me to get what it wanted. My feelings were unimportant, something I wouldn't need any longer. I was raw material, sustenance for an unquenchable hunger. I was food. It ate until there was nothing left, until Megan was gone and only it remained.

Everything went away.

Nothing came back.

When I opened my eyes they weren't my eyes, they were *hers,* my new dark *friend,* the only thing I had left. I was someone else, lying down and looking at a ceiling, but not really. It looked different; it wasn't really a ceiling at all. Everything seemed impossible, glowing and blurred, otherworldly. When I moved my tongue I tasted acid, pungent and sour, disgusting and delicious. My entire mouth throbbed. I could feel it changing. There were things growing inside, dangerous things. Everything tingled. I moved my fingers and my bones felt light, almost hollow. Somehow I managed to lift what I thought was my arm, almost without weight, so fragile. I think I turned my head and breathed a thickness with no resemblance to air. I tried to sit.

A hand fell to chest, voice so distant. "No. Not yet."

I didn't question, couldn't even if I wanted to. My insides weren't ready. My voice hadn't been born again. *She* was still working her way through me, slowly taking over. It went on like this for days, maybe weeks—no way of knowing. During this period I was only half aware of my existence, of the comforting hand insisting I remain immobile and the voice telling me everything would be *okay*. Eventually the world began to crystallize and sharpen, transforming into what it would forever be. There was a pain in my belly, so deep: a *hunger* unlike anything I'd felt. I wanted to eat. I needed to eat. The sensation was so overwhelming it ripped me from my slumber, from the last bit of *sleep* I'd ever have. My eyes opened to a blinding bright whiteness, impossibly hot. My hands went to my face, fingers to straining eyes.

Someone snagged my wrist, pulled them away. "No, you need to look."

I struggled for a moment, instinctively fighting, but ultimately relented. I should have kept fighting. It hurt, pain so terrible I wanted to scream.

The voice again, "It'll get better. Give it a moment. Just a minute more."

As promised, the agony dulled, a dull throb. Maybe I just became accustomed to it. That's when I saw him, the holder of my arms and the keeper of the voice. It was *Andrew*. Behind him, the walls looked more like walls, different but recognizable. I was adjusting, beginning to make sense of things. I'd seen the room before, or one like it.

Andrew smiled a strange *biter* smile that had no place alongside his distorted features. "There. That's better, isn't it?"

He let go of my hands and I noticed them. Not mine exactly. The fingers were longer, distorted, stretched obscenely, boney knuckles and graying skin. They were gaudy things, revolting. They couldn't be mine.

Please don't let them be mine.

When I tried to move them, they responded, hints of muscle visible below the skin, nails already

stretching, curling to a point. They *were* my hands.
They were also *hers*. *She* coiled the disgusting things
into fists. *She* punched *Andrew* in his ugly face. I rolled
from the half-broken cot with *her* to the floor,
freakish arms flailing, lanky and awkward. When we
screamed, we screamed together, voice like thunder,
the wail of a *thing,* of a *beast*. *Andrew* fell on top of us,
wrestling us to the ground, screaming for us to relax
with his disgusting mouth and horrible teeth. Two
more *biters* entered the room. A bony knee fell to our
chest, another to our neck. Foul hands grabbed our
ankles, pinning them to the stone.

Andrew wailed, pleading. "Stop it! Stop!"

To our left was a door; *biter* heads peeked in, eyes
wide, each uglier than the last. We wanted them to
leave. We wanted them to go away, crawl back to
their hole in the ground and stay there, where they
belonged. I wanted to cry. I wanted to sob
uncontrollably until there was nothing left, until the
world folded in again and went away. *She* wasn't
capable of crying, of making tears.

We would never cry again.

Days passed. In that time my body continued to
change. My limbs narrowed and stretched and my
back began to twist: the beginnings of a hunch. So
many teeth emerged. In no time at all there were rows
of them, new ones sprouting by the hour, stretching

further into the recesses of my mouth. The color in my eyes turned to soup, milky and vague. I didn't sleep, not any more. Everything felt different. Everything took longer, time elongating like my body, distorting. I felt lighter, faster. When I walked, I crept on silent feet, always listening, hearing it all. Often I found myself fighting the urge to drop to all fours, move like something decidedly inhuman. I wasn't human anymore. I was *her*. *She* was me. We were a *monster*.

We were a *biter*.

I learned to live among them in the ruins of our underground shelter, always hungry, always hurting. I had no choice. I kept to myself, away from the group, found the closest thing to a closet, and moved inside. I liked it there; it was the only thing that felt familiar. Occasionally, *Andrew* would try to talk to me. Sitting outside my door, he'd tell me things I'd need to know, about what I'd become and what I'd have to do.

"It's not easy, Megan. It will never be easy again."

I almost thought he was joking. It had never been easy.

When he said I'd have to eat, I shuddered. "Go away."

I didn't recognize my voice.

Every day *Andrew* returned and talked as I listened. He told me about his family, about his life before he changed and the things he'd left behind. He was more open about those days than anyone I'd met. He'd been a *biter* for a decade, from the onset of the fire, since the day everything changed. He'd accepted what he'd become. At the same time he refused to forget what he'd been.

I asked him the one question I needed answered. "What happened to *Blueeyes?*"

Andrew was confused; it took him a moment to realize who I was talking about. "Oh. He…he just left."

For the second time in weeks, I died. My chin fell to my chest and my already cracked voice cracked again. "I-I…why?"

It was a while before *Andrew* responded. "He didn't say…just told me to tell you *no more, Megans.*"

Blueeyes had watched two of us die, Megans. He failed us and it was more than he could bear. When I inhaled, I could still smell him, could almost see him when I closed my eyes. I'd smelled him when I went to sleep and woke again: an aftertaste, a lingering memory of something I used to be. Despite everything *she* took from me, *she* never took that.

Andrew would later explain that it was normal, that we all remembered the last thing we smelled before dying. He said it would never go away. For years he'd smelled nothing but raspberries; he sounded broken when he told me. I didn't know what they were. I felt sorry for him.

Andrew put his hand to the door. I could hear his fingers, twisted nails dragging against wood. "I'm sorry, Megan."

"So am I."

More time passed; not sure how much, and I can't say I cared. The day came when I left my closet and began to move among them. They terrified me, the way they moved, the blank eyes staring. When I looked at them I saw *monsters*. When they looked at me they saw one of their own. The strange way they spoke began to make sense: whispers and blurry words, everything stretched. I didn't want to understand them, to speak or move like them. I didn't want to be there anymore. I needed to leave.

It was night when I snuck through *Andrew's* laboratory and into the well *Blueeyes* and I had used to escape. I climbed the broken ladder, lifted the grate, and returned to the outside world for the first time. I had no plan, nowhere to go. I just wanted to run and keep running until I knew they wouldn't find me. The world outside looked different, felt different. The night was so bright, so incredibly clear. Everything seemed transparent, ghostly. I could see through the trees and for miles in every direction. When I looked at the sky, I looked past the clouds. I saw stars, so many stars, so beautiful: hints of colors I didn't know existed. I could hear everything. The wind was clear, smooth, like the surface of a frozen lake. My senses shimmered.

"What are you doing, Megan?" It was *Andrew*. "You shouldn't be out here, not yet."

At that moment I could have run. He might not have followed. If he had, I could have fought back. I might have escaped.

I didn't run, didn't move.

When I inhaled, I smelled *Blueeyes*. His scent hung from the trees, saturated the earth, rolled with the winds. My friend was right when he said this was my world. I wasn't *Andrew*, didn't have stories of *better days*. There were no fond remembrances. There was no point in running. Life had always been hard and always would be. I could adapt. I was born in this place, twice.

Andrew extended his hand. "Come back inside."

This was my world and I needed to start acting like it.

If *Blueeyes* was out there, I would find him; wouldn't stop until I did. I needed him to know he hadn't failed me, and was one of the few I'd ever trusted. I needed him to know how much he meant. I had his scent. It wasn't much, a *crumb*.

It would have to be enough.

AVAILABLE FALL 2014

ABOUT THE AUTHOR

Steven Novak is a writer, illustrator, graphic designer and lover of all things full-blown nerdy and vaguely nerd-related. He has designed over two hundred covers for independent authors across the globe and currently resides in southern California with his wife. *Megan* is the first novel in the *Breadcrumbs For The Nasties* series. More of his work can be found at **www.novakillustration.com**